LIVING IN THE SHADOW OF THE CROSS
The Gospel According To Archangel Gabriel

Dorothy Davies

LIVING IN THE SHADOW OF THE CROSS
The Gospel According To Archangel Gabriel

Fiction4All

A FICTION4ALL PAPERBACK

ISBN: 978-1-904086-65-9

Fiction4All
www.fiction4all.com

This Edition
Published 2016

Dedication

This book is dedicated with great affection and grateful thanks to the Reverend Richard Watson and Mrs Watson. We lost touch many years ago when I moved away from the parish of Hornchurch in Essex. I believe he was promoted to Bishop and also moved away.

He was a tower of strength at a time when I needed a tower more than anything and his wife was a true shoulder, never ever making me feel I was a burden on them. I have never forgotten their kindness, their comfort and their unshakeable faith. I will be forever grateful for the support at a time when it was so needed. If anyone reading this book knows where they are, perhaps they would let them know they are remembered. If Revd. and Mrs Watson would like to get in touch, I will send them my thanks for the support at the time when I was walking in the wilderness, just as He did. I used to think mine was man-made …

Special thanks go to:

Mary Holliday, devoted friend

Ann-Jacqueline for the stunning soul portrait of Gabriel

Terry Wakelin because he is Terry Wakelin, my rock and my anchor as always

My Inner Circle for support, love, laughter, guidance and for always being there.

Gabriel has asked that a percentage of royalties be allocated to charity from his book be sent to the Earl Mountbatten Hospice here on the Isle of Wight.

***

He lived just 33 earth years in his last reincarnation.

In that time he changed the lives of many hundreds – since that time he has changed the lives of countless millions.

He is known by many names – in your movement you call him the Master Jesus or the Nazarene.

Gabriel

***

'In the beginning' is a good start to any story and many have written and rewritten accounts of accounts until there are so many contradictions that man has diversified into numerous different religions based upon their interpretation of the rewritten word.

What saddens Spirit is man's inability to accept other's points of view. Jesus was Spirit Personified. He attempted to explain the peace of Spirit and that all are equal within. It does not matter how Jesus died, or when. What matters is that He came and He laid the foundation of our belief and this most important fact has sadly been lost in man's greed, selfishness and ignorance.

White Water (guide and teacher)

***

One Solitary Life

Here is a man who was born in an obscure village, the child of a peasant woman. He grew up in another obscure village. He worked in a carpenter's shop until he was thirty, and then for three years was a travelling preacher. He never wrote a book. He never had an office. He never owned a home. He never had a family. He never went to college. He never put his foot inside a big city. He never went two hundred miles from the place where he was born. He never did one of the things that usually accompany greatness. He had no credentials but himself. While still a young man, the tide of popular opinion turned against him. His friends ran away. One of them denied him. He was turned over to his enemies. He went through the mockery of a trial. He was nailed to a cross between two thieves. His executioners gambled for the only piece of property he had on earth while he was dying – and that was his coat. When he was dead, he was taken down and laid in a borrowed grave through the pity of a friend.

Twenty wide centuries have come and gone and today he is the cornerstone of the human race and the keystone of the Kingdom of God.

When I say that all the armies that ever marched, and all the navies that were ever built and all the parliaments that ever sat, and all the kings that have ever reigned, have not affected the life of man as powerfully as that "One Solitary Life" – none will be found to disagree.

Author unknown.

Introduction and Explanation

I was brought up in a time when children were required to attend Sunday School and was confirmed into the Church of England at the age of twenty one: its rituals, hymns and prayers are stamped into my psyche like a stick of rock. But … for the sixteen years before I left the Church, I only attended 8 AM Holy Communion. I love the 1662 Common Prayer service; it is full of beautiful silences, stately prayers and incantations; no hymns at all.

I have been a member of the Spiritualist movement for the past sixteen years, working with Spirit and being directed by them in all I do.

Spiritualists have put different words to the old hymn tunes. Spiritualist hymns are the ones I have sung at services during many of those years. You can doubtless imagine my bemusement, therefore, when I spent the best part of two days singing: "When I survey the wondrous Cross/on which the Prince of Glory died". In desperation I finally said; "All right, Spirit, why am I singing this hymn?" The answer was one that surprised me. I should be used to surprises from Spirit but...

Many years ago I wrote the 'story' of the life of Jesus of Nazareth, leaving out the parables and preaching, simply combining the four Gospels into one long story. I called it "Living In The Shadow Of The Cross", a quote taken from the writings of a medieval monk who wrote: "Life is but a shadow cast by the Cross." Lay people were deeply moved by the manuscript, publishers and clerics were not so taken with it. The project was abandoned. The book was destroyed and all but forgotten.

Then a fellow employee bought me an Angel book for Christmas. I didn't get very far with it, not wanting to use it as an oracle, but I did follow the instructions to find out the name of my guardian angel. Surprise No. 1. My guardian angel is Gabriel.

So when I asked the question about the hymn, an angel tapped me on the shoulder and said, in response to my question about the hymn: "I want you to write that book again, but from a different perspective, from my perspective. I, who walked the earth plane with him, know the truth and want to give the truth to the people to read. And by the way, you can use the same title, for it would be hard to find a better one."

It had to be Gabriel, for he had been very close for some time. I had seen him guarding our circle and our meeting place and once crashing into my meditation, complaining about his wings, demanding to know why us earth people visualise angels with wings. He insists they are the most cumbersome and difficult things to cope with, especially when it comes to negotiating doorways. Gabriel, you will quickly appreciate, has the most delightful and wry sense of humour as well as deep sensitivity and wisdom as befits an Archangel.

But I confess here that the answer to my question was Surprise No. 2.

I am glad to say the hymn shifted itself out of my mind after this conversation: it was becoming a little tedious! I gave a lot of thought to the title and yes, it is appropriate, more than it was back then when I wrote the first book. Now I understand so much more. I know that when Jesus made the decision to come to earth, he came knowing his destiny. Therefore his entire short life was lived in the shadow of the Cross, aware of the fate that was to be his.

With the usual way of Spirit, push-tug-direct-push a little more, there happened to be an excellent series on TV at the time the book began, one which looked at the historical background to his life. It helped a lot to make sense of Gabriel's words. I watched every episode and wish to send thanks to Jeremy Bowen for the even-handed, unbiased way he presented a very complex and often tricky subject.

The book was started but when it seemed it wasn't going fast enough, there came another gentle push. There was a basket of cheap CDs for sale in the local newsagents. The top one, left waiting for me to see, was by The Edwin Hawkins Singers, featuring "Oh Happy Day."

'Oh happy day, oh happy day, when Jesus walked...'

Have you seen swan feathers? They look as if they had come from an angel's wing. There are swan feathers lying in my fireplace as I write this, given to me as a gift.

Hints, pushes, feelings, touches on shoulder and head. All there, all real, all pushing me on.

So, with a much treasured New Testament on the desk, (to check information and spelling - Gabriel laughed at me every time I did it), I put earphones on to listen to totally peaceful New Age music from talented musicians and composers. This helped me to shut out the world and allowed me to leave myself open to translate Gabriel's words into script. With wildly tingling hands, I opened up to my angel and began once again to rewrite the life of the Nazarene, the man I once called Saviour and whom I now call friend.

Here then is the Gospel According To the Archangel Gabriel.

Dorothy Davies, Isle of Wight,
in the Year of Our Lord, 2011.

The words of the Archangel Gabriel

Foreword

In the Realms, we as individual souls live and are in contact with one another on many different levels: psychic, telepathic, totally spiritual. It is a world of so much beauty that, if you were to see it, none of you would want to stay on the earth plane a single moment longer than you had to. And that is no word of a lie! That is why you are only shown glimpses of Heaven, as you term it, for there would be so many wanting to go home if they knew the truth that none would be left to cope with those who have no understanding of this great truth. Imagine: the glory of the Summerlands revealed to all – what great waves there would be of people taking their own lives to get there. That is not the Great Divine Plan. The earth you inhabit is one of learning and you are there to learn. But know that there are glories beyond imagination on the other side of the veil. Know that those who have had what you term a Near Death Experience are restless, never entirely content when they return to your side, for they were called – pulled by the light and yet it was not their time so they had to return. But in returning they took with them a hint of what it was like and what it would be like and it is always there, a haunting memory, something that in the darkness of night comes back to fill them with joy and desire to be there.

We use them as ambassadors for Heaven. The channel we are using for this book is recalling a time when a spirit guide said 'ghosts' were actually spirits who are earth bound by choice, they are there to encourage the disbeliever, the sceptic, into exploring your movement further. It is a matter of opinion, one that meets with approval if not with overwhelming acceptance by the rest of us, but it does well as a metaphor. We use those who experience Near Death in the same manner, if you wish to look at it that way.

***

Let me start at the start.

The time had come. We were called to a convention, for want of a better word. The Higher Beings, the ones you know as Angels, were called together to be informed of a special and significant fact.

A soul was preparing to return to earth. A delicate soul and yet one tough enough to withstand the rigours of life on the earth plane for it is no easy task, walking the earth with all that humanity has to throw at anyone, be they normal or otherwise. And this was no normal soul. This was an advanced soul, one who had been back many, many times before, but who had one last task to fulfil. Because He was returning this last time with so much to do, He was to return surrounded by helpers, guides and angels.

It is one of those angels who is relating this account to you, via the channel, at this time.

Angels have written books before via channels, not always declaring that it is so, sometimes hiding behind the names of saints, or of other people. But more and more angels are 'coming out' and declaring who they are, what they are and demanding that people take notice of them. Angel power is being accepted, angels are recognised for what they are, beings of light who have much to give: wisdom, guidance, love, protection and joy. Angels are known to many different religions and many different peoples, we have many names but the constant theme in the descriptions is that of light. It is this light which made the early artists depict us as having haloes, which is a representation of our auras, of course. We don't need wings to fly but they could not conceive of people flying without them, so we have wings. And if we wish to appear to you in a form you can understand and accept, we come with wings. Sometimes they get in the way, for we aren't used to them really and the folding and unfolding of so many feathers is not as easy as it looks. But we persevere – Angels are not easily put off.

This angel has had to fight quite hard to gain acceptance with his channel, for the usual disbelief comes in: 'why me, is it real, is it my imagination, why have I been chosen, am I good enough, can I do the job' and back again to 'is it real?' My answer, then and now: *I have walked with you since you arrived on this earth plane. I chose you for many reasons, not least of which are the skills I knew you would acquire. You were chosen in part for your channelling experience. It is real; it is not your imagination. You are good enough or you would not have been given the work. You can do the job and yes, it is real.*

Such a convention of angels had never been seen before in the Realms: every higher being attended before the Godhead, the Great White Spirit of Love. His radiance outshone every one of us put together and we were a mass of pure radiance, believe me. We outshone your sun many times over and yet he was brighter and more radiant than all of us. The one who was to return was stood with him, his Chosen One.

And we were told this one was to be a messenger, to bring the truth to those who would hear. We were told in advance that his ministry would not be easy but would be life changing for all who came into contact with it. We were to walk with him every step of the way to ensure no harm came to the Great Plan, we had to ensure that what was ordained took place. For only that way would the will of the Great White Spirit of Love come into effect.

I said "I will walk with him for all time."

Raphael, my dear friend, said "I will walk with Him for all time."

Others said they would walk for a time and then make way for others.

And the Godhead said that is exactly what he hoped we would say and the angels concerned were the ones he hoped would say it. So this one sat with us and we talked of the work he had ahead.

We were agreed on certain things in advance: he would not be born to a rich family, for it would make it harder to leave them and go out into the world with the message He had to preach. Although it might be good for a soul to have the serious temptation of wealth, it was a complication He could well do without. So, a simple family, with little money but enough to get by. The reverse of wealth is poverty and that would have put its own strain on the life to be.

Where then was the best place to spread this message of love and hope for the future, the truth of the Godhead and all that awaits everyone who makes the transition to the Realms – the cold realms of the earth plane or the warmer ones? In the end we chose the warmer climes, the better to preach outside when the time came. Cold realms put their own inhibitions on people, both those who would serve and those who would come to listen. Such was our reasoning, the discussions which flowed from one angel to another in the circle in which we sat, with the one in the centre, listening, adding some words here and there, always with a smile for each of us. We all knew this one was a being higher than ourselves and we accorded him all honour because of this and yet he sat at the same level as us; just in the centre of the circle. He was always courteous and charming, kind and gentle, always at pains to ensure we never felt he was above us even though we knew he was. We sat and we talked for half an eternity, discussing this one's new life and the problems he would come up against and how we would be able to help resolve them.

The reason for the return of a special messenger at that time was because the great Godhead felt that the people on the earth plane were in conflict with one another to a point when something had to be done, some unifying process had to take place. From your perspective, you who read this in the 21st century, you will look at that statement with disbelief and say "but since that time, mankind has fought wars over religion, killed millions in the name of religion. It has been responsible for more suffering, more pain, more heartbreak and more annihilation of peoples on this earth than any other single thing."

And I say to you in return, had he not come, had the religions not formed themselves and given men reason to fight one another, they would have found other reasons to fight one another! Land, property, people, especially females, animals – you name it, they would have fought over it and the wars would have been as bitter, as vicious, as soul searing as the ones over religion. What then is the difference between religious wars and non-religious wars? There is none. But – the coming together of people to worship, to praise, to create the most beautiful and hallowed music in his name, to make processions through towns, to erect huge buildings and then maintain them – this is an outpouring of love. And that is the key which was missing and would have been missing from the wars and the fights and the misery caused by the conflicts had He not come. He brought Love to the earth plane and we have watched you bask in that Love ever since.

Too simple an answer? My channel says 'too simple an answer, Gabriel!' and maybe it seems that way. For the world you have built is complex: it is hard for some of us to understand the devious ways of man toward his brother, hard for us to follow the technology you invent faster than your minds can learn to cope with it, for we have no need of such things and as such stand back in amazement as you create machines to do what our minds can do. But then we have to remind ourselves that you are earthbound and we are not.

But taking all that into consideration: the complex world you have built, its many layers of class, creed, caste, levels of wealth – I could go on, taking all that into consideration, we still say that the greatest mover and shaker of all is Love. What made Mother Teresa go to the poor and help them? What makes missionaries, no matter how misguided, go to the native people and try to convert them? What makes churches open their doors to the poor and lonely, what makes men give up livelihoods and study the words of the Book of Life, to become preachers and vicars and clerics? What makes men renounce the charms of women to take on the chaste role of the priesthood? What makes devoted people contribute money and time and energy to helping the parish? And in whose name are these things done?

I rest my case.

In the Beginning

In the beginning was a world ready for Love to come in human form. We were ready; we of the Realms who had chosen to walk with this soul. He was ready, having spent much time in serious deliberation and discussion with the great white Spirit of Love that this is what he really wanted to do. And the Godhead said, whilst we were there, 'you shall be as my son and I shall be as your father and I will be with you and watch over you and walk with you all the way, as will these guardian angels. But what happens to you will happen and I am not able to take from you one single part of it."

And he said: "I understand. So be it." Then he stood up and came over to each of us and took our hands and we felt the surge of energy and love that came from him and we knew he was indeed the Blessed One and that none other could take on this role, not even the higher beings, the angelic beings above us. His series of incarnations were such that it had brought him to this point, a time of pure understanding, of knowledge beyond that of any 'normal' soul.

We left the great Godhead, all of us together, those who would walk some of the time, those who would walk all of the time and we went to the centre where we could talk of who was to bring this new soul into the world. We had chosen the place, we had chosen the time; we had but to choose the person.

He spoke of a young woman, newly betrothed, virginal, innocent, yet strong in her soul for she too had walked the earth plane many times and would carry the burden well, the burden of bringing this soul into the world and seeing it depart again for we all knew that He would not live out a 'normal' earth span of life. And so we walked with him to the point of departure, the point at which a soul leaves the Realms to return to the earth plane, we surrounded him with our great light and love and he drew in that which we were able to give – strength.

The young woman was much in love with her betrothed and they had known one another, secretly, passionately and it was easy for us to arrange that this soul was the one she would conceive. The time in which they lived was a time of great strictness and lack of understanding for that which was natural and normal for the human beings to do and the fact of the child would have made life very difficult for the chosen one. So two angels visited the earth plane, one to the young woman and the other to her betrothed.

There we passed on the message that the child to come was of God, that he would be a leader, a great teacher and that no shame attached to her for carrying this child. Such was the love they had for each other that a marriage was swiftly arranged and completed and all was in order. The young woman, called Mary, was filled with heavenly love at our visit and knew, deep within her motherly heart, that this would be no ordinary child. For Mary it did not seem an odd or strange thing that an angel should visit her and give her this information but for her betrothed, Joseph, it was indeed a strange thing and for a long time he found it hard to accept our visit and our words, although he believed. We were aware how he struggled with the vision long into the dark nights, until the understanding finally came to him - he indeed had been chosen for a special task and he, like so many before – and since – said, Why Me? And we said, impressing him with our thoughts, that he was a strong man and would give this new one the right upbringing to help him be strong in the work that lay ahead.

The two talked and walked together much during the time of the pregnancy, Mary calm as always, serene as always and we watched over her, taking good care to be around her all the time, for the one she carried was the most precious of all the lives that had come into this world before – or since. It is so hard to convey to you, the reader, how precious this soul was, how wise, how all-knowing, how much he had brought to this current incarnation from all the previous times he had walked the earth plane, the knowledge he had drawn unto himself. And around them at this time the violence of man was bubbling under the surface, waiting once more to be disastrously thrown into this world once again, bringing sorrow and anguish in its wake once more. You on the earth plane know of the Four Horsemen of the Apocalypse but how many know of those who follow in the wake of the horses … the steeds of grief, anguish, untold pain and sorrow?

From the Realms, let me say that your historians insist there was no census at the time of the envisaged birth of the one. Let me say that there was such a local census and the family were required to attend another place for the counting of people. And so they went, travelling slowly and carefully on a borrowed donkey, a carpenter does not use a donkey for every day travelling, for Mary was far gone with her earthly pregnancy. It was one that had not troubled her overmuch, no sickness, no pains, nothing but the quiet acceptance that this was no ordinary child and her role in his life was to be no ordinary role. We knew, although she did not, that she too was a soul who had walked this earth plane many times in the past, as had Joseph himself. With ancient knowledge comes modern understanding and acceptance of what is, not what might be. There is a difference and the difference makes a world of chaos seem more acceptable.

The family they went to stay with had others staying too, the house was crowded and really there was no room for a wife about to give birth among so many males crammed into the place. So she was laid downstairs, with the animals, where her privacy was assured, her dignity intact and, with her husband by her side, in a small town known as Bethlehem, he came into the world as a tiny helpless child, crying his displeasure at leaving the safety and comfort of the womb.

Do I shatter a few myths here? I doubt it. The so-called Nativity story, which you have known for so many years, is in fact an amalgam of many different aspects of the same basic story – it is the translation which has changed it for the Western world.

So we go back and we tell it as it was.

There was no room in the house where they were to stay for a pregnant woman about to give birth, for the males of the family did not want to know of such things. So Mary was given a place in the animals' quarters below, clean enough, warm enough and secure enough, with the warmth of the animals themselves, away from prying eyes, with her relative to wash and tend to her and the child when he was born.

The shepherds? Oh they came. They came because one of them, watching over the flock, unable to sleep, was what you would now refer to as mediumistic. He 'saw' angelic beings hovering over the small town. He did not understand they were there, we were there to guard the child, but he thought they were messengers of great happenings. So Raphael and a couple of others went to the shepherd and told him of the child which had come and he roused the others and told them to come and see this special child. We did not say 'come and worship him' but they did anyway. And poor bemused Mary, tired from giving birth and happy that it was over, lying there with her son in her arms, did not understand these poor shepherds who came to stand and stare and who told her of the vision one had seen and how this child would be special. That she knew, of course, but this was her proof. You always want proof and she had hers, in this fashion.

Days of recuperation, days of living upstairs and sleeping downstairs, for still the family were there, the family who ooh-ed and aah-ed over the new-born child and said how fortunate they were to have a boy child as the first one, so much better for the family line. Joseph and Mary exchanged quiet smiles of knowingness, telling no-one about the angels. After all, the shepherds had done enough 'damage' with their talk to keep half of Bethlehem going…

But, when all seemed quiet and normal again, the travellers arrived in the town, asking about the new-born child.

Psychics to a man, astrologers by trade, astronomers in their spare time, the three wise men (for wise they were, beyond their years, old souls returned for another incarnation) came to see the One they knew had arrived. Their story was they had followed a star, a nova which had flared at the time of his birth, which they took as a sign of a new King come to the earth. Foreign they were, with dark skins, black beards and strangely coloured robes of a kind not seen in this part of the world. From beneath heavy cloaks they brought out their gifts: gold, frankincense and myrrh.

Two thousand years on, it is easy for the people to say 'oh of course they brought these gifts, gold for a King, frankincense and myrrh, priceless perfumes and oils to anoint him and if myrrh had overtones of death and tombs, well, it just went to show…' but it wasn't like that. Gold was a commodity, a currency where these men came from and the expensive oils were a gift for a lady who had borne a special child. 'Hindsight is 20-20 vision' is a saying current in the modern world and it is indeed a truth when it comes to the life of this special one, for you have, can and do read all manner of things into the happenings of that time.

All the same the gifts were prophetic, for the wise men told Mary, in stumbling speech for her language was not theirs, that the child was born to be King. If they knew of his ultimate fate, they were not saying, for it was not a good thing to say to a young mother with her first child in any event. More proof for Mary. And another layer to add to the subsequent legend of his life.

After the congratulations, the gift giving and the surprise of having such strangers come visiting, came the bad news. Always there is bad news; it is a rule of life! In their search for the child, they had gone to the Palace of Herod, ruler of the whole area, and asked his advisers if they knew where the Child who would be King had been born. With honey dripping from their mouths, the advisers said they knew of no King, but if the great men found where he was, would they call back and tell them so they could in turn tell their King and he could go and worship him. But the eyes told a different story and the wise men, not being quite so wise outside their own country, knew they had made a serious mistake. So they promised and the moment they left the palace they had a hasty conference as they hurried away and agreed, whatever happened, they would go back home another way.

It took them a further week to find him, following the directions picked up from talking with people in the inns and hostels where they stayed overnight, for the talk of the shepherds and their visitation by angels was all over the area. By asking discreet questions and deducing the answers, the wise men came at last to Bethlehem and there found the baby and his mother, just as everyone said they would.

Be warned, they told the family, Herod will not stand for anyone in line for his position in life.

After the wise men had left, going a long way around the palace so the spies, the underground movement all rulers set up to cover themselves, would not notice their passing, Mary and Joseph gathered their few things together, said goodbye to the family who had housed them, got the now fat and lazy donkey from the stable and set off back to Nazareth, where they hoped to be safe.

If they had but known how their fears were unnecessary and unjustified! Angels walked with them every step of the way, angels guarded them against footpads and robbers of all kinds, angels cast a spell of darkness over the gold and precious spices so none would catch a glimpse of the gifts and try to take them. Angels cast a spell of protection over the family as they made their way back home, full of happiness at their baby and the life they hoped to have. And at that time, we have to say, the future seemed bright for Mary, she had put from her mind all thought of his becoming a great leader, for leaders usually put themselves in the firing line and that was something she could not and did not contemplate. But then she was young, very much in love and a first time mother. Why should she think on such things? Why should there be clouds on her horizon?

If they had known then of the vengeance of Herod, deprived of the knowledge he sought, the birth of someone said to be King, there would have been clouds indeed. If they had known that every firstborn son would be killed by Herod's men then there would have been sorrow enough for Mary to burden her for the rest of her life. But she was spared this knowledge, for in that time news did not spread outside of a region and only those who suffered in the area knew of the terrible wrath of the terrible man.

***

I am mentioned in the Gospels as being the angel who visited Simeon, Mary and everyone else, apparently. Well, a name is a name is a name and an angel is an angel is an angel after all, although I have to say Raphael does feel rather left out at times. It was in fact he who visited Mary and Joseph and I who backed up the message of the wise men for the Family to get out of Bethlehem fast. It was I who visited Simeon in the temple and arranged for his wife to give birth to John, later known as John the Baptist, another great man with a destiny that had to be fulfilled. After I made the startling statement to Simeon, another angel took over and guarded that soul as and when it came back to earth through its life and to its well-publicised but necessary death.

On the subject of death, as the word has just crept into this book, I would like to say to all who read these words that the children who were slaughtered by Herod's men are all alive and well and grown up into aged and wise souls here in the Realms. They had their destiny, they fulfilled it and all returned home. The reason is one known to the great Godhead and is not for us lesser mortals to know, but it was to be and it was.

Early Years

Scholars have written their thoughts, saints have added their contributions, priests often speculate but no one – apart from he who lived through it and we who walked with him – know of those early years. There is not much to say about that time: He grew up in a loving caring environment with his brothers and sister, he had caring relatives and adoring doting parents who did everything good Jewish families should do: observed the laws of the land and of their religion, observing the Sabbath with strict formality and carrying out all the rituals on the right days at the right time. So he grew in a family of great faith and adherence to the laws, went to the synagogue to hear the rabbi preach on the Scriptures and the Word of God and inside he knew he was different but could not let anyone know.

He became a studious boy, seeking to learn all that was to be learned. He became an adept carpenter at Joseph's side, loving the feel of the wood and the smell of the sawdust as timber was shaped and cut and put together. He learned the laws and recited the prayers. He also played with other children and at times was indistinguishable from them in a crowd. Then there would come a moment, a pause as it were, when he would stop and gaze into the far distance, seeing things no others saw, hearing things no others heard. What he saw and what he heard we did not know, we who guarded him, but we knew he had seen something and heard something. The gift was developing even then. You would see him tip his head to one side, listening and sometimes looking as if he was on the point of answering someone but then his lips would clamp shut and if he answered them, it was with his mind, not aloud when others might or could hear.

His presentation at the Temple was a turning point in his young life. The full force of the Jewish law appeared to descend on him at that time; he became more solemn, more withdrawn. Many noticed and commented on it; many times he was called to play but did not go, sitting instead under a shady tree and contemplating the far horizon, lost in meditation. None disturbed him at that time, they seemed to know, to understand or sense that something was going on. It helped that we stood guard, too, an invisible barrier to protect him when he went away in his mind, for it was dangerous for him to be disturbed, so deep was his contemplation and meditation. Sometimes he would look at us and smile and we knew he had seen us, for the smile was so full of understanding and acceptance that it could have meant nothing else. And we would smile back, for he was a soul to be loved, cherished and treasured above all others.

Much is made in the Gospel of the time when the family went to Jerusalem for the Passover and how he stayed behind to talk to the learned men. We who walked with him did not find this strange although his loving anxious parents did. We knew of his insatiable appetite for knowledge and for learning of all kinds. We also knew that he was developing fast and the classic lines he spoke at that time were truthfully related to the Gospel writer.

"Did you not know that I was bound to be in my Father's house?"

In essence he was saying to Mary and Joseph that this is my true home, this is where I ought to be, worshipping the God Jehovah and sharing the services of these great learned men. But he was only twelve years old and had more living to do before he could do such a thing. So it was with great reluctance he went with them, back to Nazareth, to carry on his life. This we know, for this he voiced to us during his meditation times, when he spoke aloud to those of us who were guarding him. He said:

"I need to worship the God, my Father."

And – "I should be at the temple, learning from the wise men."

And – "I should be about my Father's business for time is short and there is much to be done."

And – "Why do you not call me to my ministry?"

And we said, as gently but firmly as we could, "the time is not yet. Your time is not yet come. Yes, there is unrest, yes there are problems, yes there is need for a leader but you are young and untested and inexperienced and we have need of you to be here right now, carrying on your studies, becoming strong in both mind and body. We will call you when the day comes. Be sure of that."

If he fully understood, we never really knew, for he said little after that, but spent his time in deep meditation as we wanted him to, so we could implant the thoughts needed to carry him forward, to take him into his ministry when the time was right. And oh, how he longed for the time to be right! But there was living to do, growing to do, for he was but a young man full of the vigour of life but without the seasoning that comes with experience – we needed him to learn to be diplomatic and tactful and learned and wise and able to argue coherently without losing the point. We needed him to learn to preach which he did by standing up and talking to the small groups which tended to surround him. People were drawn to him and he spoke to them, gently, firmly, putting his point of view across.

And so he developed and we stood back and knew he was following the path, albeit reluctantly, of patient waiting and development.

During this time his mother began to realise fully what an extraordinary child she had brought into the world. She would watch him at his meditations and studies, would call to Joseph quietly and say: "Look at our son, how intense he is, how he studies!"

Joseph would nod and agree and say: "He is special but we knew that from the start, beloved one."

"Yes," she agreed, "but I had no idea how special."

And she took great care to keep from the other children how she favoured the son she called Jesus, for there should be no jealousy and no animosity among siblings. But they too knew that this older brother was different, that he had a different outlook on life to them, that he spent more time in studies and in deep thought – they did not appreciate at that time that it was meditation – something they could not understand.

At times Mary, the beloved Mother, would look round quickly as if she had caught sight of us, maybe heard the rustle of a wing or the soft sound of our robes as we passed her by. She had some powers of psychic awareness but, knowing her place in society, never sought to develop them, even though she could have done. It was enough, we believe, for her to know that someone or something was there, always around the beloved son.

And so he grew in stature and in ability, he grew in experience of the world. He did not scorn women but did not seek their company, either, even though they sought him out and spent time looking at him with longing eyes for he was handsome of face and strong of body and carried this aura of mystery around him which none could understand but all were drawn to. He sought no woman for his own; no one claimed his time or his thoughts in that way. Always the thoughts were turned toward the future, the ministry which was ahead of him. He could not have remembered at that time the death which awaited him but there was a sense of darkness around his mind when meditating on the future, when sending out thoughts for the way to be shown to him. It was this which seemed to held him back from making a relationship with a woman, for it would have meant commitment which maybe he felt he would not have wanted to break or if he did, there would be heartache for them both and that would have got in the way of the pathway He was to walk.

It is a shame that the priests who have followed him have taken a vow of chastity to follow in his footsteps for they do not have the same reasons as he did for doing just this. They have no great mission to accomplish; they are not ground breaking as he was. Their task is to serve their flocks, to be a nurturer of souls, to marry those who wish to enter into wedded bliss and baptise the union of that wedded bliss and put safely back into the earth, in whatever form, those who depart the earth plane. Their task is to be comforters and advisers and this they could do from the sanctuary of marriage but because he chose that route, so they must follow. But it is not necessary, for as I said, they do not walk his path, nor could they, for his was a solitary life in many ways. For sure there were friends and there was family but he had a vision and he had to follow it to its terrible tragic conclusion. How much was in his mind we never really knew, for we did not intrude on his thoughts. We did not seek to know what he thought but were there to impress our strength on him and encourage him and be with him so that he would not be lonely.

In this we succeeded but oh! The path for him was a tormented one!

The Call

When he had walked the earth plane for thirty years, he finally heard the call he had been waiting for. In that time – and many times since on the earth plane – a travelling preacher appears in a town or city, exhorting all to come and be baptised in the name of God or the Holy Spirit or whatever. You know them, you have heard them or seen them on your televisions and in great arenas. At that time they came to river-sides and called the population to them. Such a one was John known as the Baptist. Wild he was, wild of hair and of body, a hairy man covered in skins and roughly made sandals. He had a long beard and long nails and wild piercing eyes that none could escape. His voice was loud and hectoring, it rang out across the countryside, it brought people running from their daily tasks for here indeed was a man of God, living on the fruits of the wilderness, the berries, the plants and the seeds and nuts of bushes. Clean of heart and mind, this man, clean of body too for when he baptised people he too was baptised in the great River Jordan. Yet people were afraid of him, afraid that he might have something they would catch because his hair was so wild and long and his nails so jagged like talons but it was only because he had endured his time in the wilderness. Some people find their spiritual guidance by sitting quietly in groups, others by sitting quietly by a tree or a stream but for John known as the Baptist the wilderness was where he walked, lived, had his being, where he communed with Spirit every waking hour of every day. Until he was strong enough to fulfil his mission, to bring people to the river, to tell them of the Messiah who was coming.

His angel often pulls a face of exasperation, almost a grimace, when he remembers how often someone said to John: "are you he who we are waiting for?" and the times John had to reply: "I am not He, He is still to come."

And still they came, hundreds of them, questions on their lips, hope in their hearts, the tyranny of oppression upon them, hoping for a Saviour, a Messiah; a leader to take them to freedom. They found the Wild Man, the locust eater, the man who had the nerve to stand up to the Pharisees and Sadducees and others who came to stand and stare and point and call him names, shouting back at them.

And so they demanded he became their Messiah.

And he said it was not his role.

And he kept on saying it until the day Jesus left his work at the bench and went to the River Jordan to see the Wild Man for himself, wondering if this was the call he had been waiting for.

Jesus stood on the river bank among the crowd who, as one, had fallen back to let him pass as the waves rolled back once for Moses and the Children of Israel to cross the Red Sea. (You still think that was a tale? Believe me, it happened! I was there, a junior angel at that time, and saw it for myself. I agree, not everything in what you call the Old Testament is true, some things are distorted, some are exaggerated, much actually happened. These were different times, special times, when so-called 'miracles' such as the parting of the Red Sea, could happen for man was closer to Spirit at that time than he is today. The power of the mind can do so much. Read the story of Daniel again, it was his powerful mind that let him and his friends walk into the lions' den. There is more, much more, but you need to read the book of life for yourself and decide what is right and what isn't, bearing in mind what I have just said.)

A small diversion. Apologies.

We were standing on the river bank, Jesus and myself, and in the water, John known as the Baptist and his angel, getting miserably wet and wondering how long the baptism game was going to last. All right, maybe angels don't get wet but his angel didn't look very happy,

I can tell you. Too many people, too many silly questions and – as we all know – a sad end not so far away. One his angel could do nothing about. Oh, let me divert again for a moment, my channel is full of questions this night.

When a soul goes home there is indeed much rejoicing. When a soul goes home because of the treachery and deceit and trickery of others, it is not so much an occasion for rejoicing, for sometimes not all the work has been completed. You are taught, rightly, that everyone goes home when they should, when it is their time (with the exception of suicides, who often have to come back and complete what they failed on this time round) and indeed John known as the Baptist had to go home at that time and in that way. But it left many sorrowing on the earth plane and a guardian angel who, whilst knowing what had to happen, still felt responsible and unhappy at the ending of a fearsome life, an awesome power, a potent prophet. That soul has come back to walk the earth plane many times since, he has been a powerful voice in many countries around this earth plane of yours, he has spoken out on many issues: coloured rights, women's rights, he has fought poverty, fought injustice, fought corruption and evil in high places, often resulting in yet another 'untimely' death – and still he returns to fight battles on behalf of mankind! Such a soul is a rarity and one that is cherished by the great Godhead himself. And yes, his angel walks with him every time.

Back to the main story again.

You need to picture this. Jesus is on the river bank, standing among the people who have parted to let Him reach the water's edge. John known as the Baptist is in the water, standing in the coolness, wet to his knees and beyond, wild hair flinging droplets of water in all directions, every one sparkling its own rainbow in the sun. And the people falling silent as one so that nothing is heard but the water itself and the birds. And the two men looked at one another across the space of water and time and they both knew that this was a momentous occasion. It seemed to shout the fact from them both. I shared a glance with John known as the Baptist's angel, one I had worked with in the past. We both shrugged our wings and stood back to let the happening happen. As we knew it would and as we knew it should.

What they said was:

"I have come to be baptised."

"It is not right and seemly, it is for you to baptise me."

"No. We both know what is right and this is right."

And John known as the Baptist shook the wild hair and the long wild beard and the skin he wore shook itself as if alive and a million droplets of water flew in all directions and for a fleeting moment that was all but frozen in time he was surrounded by a living moving rainbow.

Still the people were silent. It was a miracle that people could be silent for so long, no sound but their breathing filling the air of the golden day when two great men came together in the great River Jordan.

With no more words, he stepped into the water and John known as the Baptist reached out for him. The touch was electric, we felt it, us angels, it quivered our wings and trembled through our bodies. John known as the Baptist's angel lit up as if by fire as John known as the Baptist caught the chosen one in his arms and lowered him into the sacred waters.

And the moment came when he came out of the water, glistening and gleaming and glowing with righteousness that a dove appeared from nowhere and landed on his shoulder and a voice spoke within the minds of everyone there – a voice so powerful that there was no way none could not have heard it:

"This is my Beloved Son, in whom I am well pleased."

John known as the Baptist looked at Jesus and smiled a sad smile. "It is done," he said.

"It is right," said Jesus and took John known as the Baptist's hands. "Fight on, fight on in the name of God." And he turned and stepped out of the water and then the spell was broken and everyone began to talk at once. The dove flew away. John known as the Baptist stood in the centre of the river watching him walk away, knowing his sadness, knowing his destiny in his own heart and knowing his own as well. He had looked into the future and it was not there. He shook more droplets from his wildness and called again for those to come and be baptised. And many flooded into the great Jordan river to be baptised by a man so closely associated with someone clearly in the favour of the great God.

Jesus stopped only long enough to send someone with a message to his mother that he was going to take some time alone and went away from Nazareth into the wilderness. The call had come and he needed to think, to meditate, to receive guidance on the way ahead. For it was not a broad path he had to walk, it was one filled with rocks and crevices, with cracks and boulders, with poisonous snakes and venomous creatures of all kind, human and animal, waiting to trap him. He had to prepare, to clear his mind and thoughts, to become a pure channel for the work ahead.

And so he went alone, undefended except for angels – a powerful protection, I have to say in my own defence and his – and without provisions of any kind. He just walked away from all civilisation. His eyes were set on the far horizon and his thoughts were in turmoil. As he walked his robe dried in the heat of the sun, creating a fine mist around him for a while and his feet became caked in dust and dirt. His hair continued to sparkle for some time, the water trapped in the darkness reflecting back the sun much as the water droplets on John known as the Baptist's hair had done earlier. The noise of the crowd diminished as he walked away, the great roar of humanity muting itself as if being gently shut down by some great hand. The rustle of animals in the bushes he passed did not disturb him. As if speaking to me he said over and over: "it has come. My time has come. This is the call. It has come. My time has come. This is the call. It has come. My time has come. This is the call." I thought at first he was trying to reassure or even convince himself that it was indeed the call he had waited for but then I realised it was a surge of energy so great that it could not be contained in that one body without some expression to the outside world. In fact he was all but marching to the mantra he chanted: measure the words. IT. HAS. COME. MY. TIME. HAS. COME. THIS. IS. THE. CALL. And step to it. It becomes a marching rhythm. And with this on his lips, he marched into the desert area.

And there he stayed for forty days.

He slept in a small cave. He washed in a small pool. He drank from the same pool. He walked many miles in great circles, arguing with himself and with God, trying to silence his mind to receive the words he knew had to come to him. He sat for hours in total stillness, chanting single word mantras, absorbing the impressions that were being given to him by those wiser than I whose task it was to fill this one with the right wisdom for the task ahead. He often slept sitting upright in meditation, falling asleep even as they channelled the thoughts into his receptive waiting mind. Even in sleep state they came to him, bringing him visions, advice, strength, knowledge and guidance. And I stood back and let them do their work for my task was to guard him at this time, to walk with him, not to interfere with the knowledge giving procedures. I had enough problems keeping away the wild animals who wanted to attack this lone person who threw no stones at them to scare them away, who sat so still they often thought he was dead and wanted to leap at him and drag the flesh from his bones. I cast rigid defences around him as he sat and he never once looked up to wonder why the animals did not cross a certain barrier around him. Perhaps he knew. Raphael was there too, helping put up defences, working at keeping the dangers out. Usually a duty shared is a duty halved but here it was so important, so critical, that we both worked flat out for the entire time he was there. Ah, poor exhausted angels. Do the Gospels mention us? Not really.

"Then the devil left him and angels appeared and waited on Him."

As if we walked in at the end and took over. Not as if we had been there, through every fraught minute and hour, through the days and weeks and cold and heat and dirt and sadness he went through.

We asked ourselves, how did they know, those Biblical writers? There was no one there with him but us.

They knew because later he told them of his struggles and how the angels were with him to help. I guess any mention is better than none at all…

In his time in the wilderness he fought many devils. The good Book says he fought but one, the Dark Angel himself, but I know better, for I was there, remember, I was there throughout. He fought many devils. The Dark Angel sent them, of course he did, for he was jealous of the love the Godhead had for this one and it would have been a great victory to have brought this one to the point when he would turn his back on the chosen path and choose riches and comfort against the rigours and certain agonising death ahead of him. But Jesus had already been filled with heavenly wisdom and knowledge, had already come to terms with his future before the Dark Angel got around to sending the dark ones to tempt him.

But temptations there were aplenty. Rock does not make a soft bed for someone who had walked many miles trying to calm a troubled mind. A soft bed would be good. Food would be better than snatched berries, wine would be better than stagnant water. Clean robes are better than ones stiff with dirt and caked in dust and which smell.

But again he knew the time when he would go back home and gain a little comfort and there were some days to go before he was ready to leave, ready to start his new pathway. Before then, he grew gaunt and weary, his eyes grew large in a face already solemn and lined with suffering which some would say was self-induced. Was it? Do we not at times all have our wilderness to walk? Fine, so yours was not a desert where wild animals stalked you and food was scarce and the ground a hard bed and a rock a hard pillow. But was it not as desolate as this as you walked through your Valley of Desolation? When tears fell freely and the agony in the heart was such that at times you did not want to wake in the morning? This was your time in the desert. However you spent it, we all go through it. For some it is a bad relationship they cannot escape. For others it is an illness they have to endure. For others it is grinding poverty, for yet more it is the rigors of prison life. Then there are those who endure the loss of a child or loved one and never get over grieving for the lost soul. So many wildernesses you humans have to endure!

I give away no secrets when I say my channel's wilderness was given to her twice: the first time she was rescued by the people she has dedicated this book to – fine people who held out the equivalent of manna from heaven to a heart and mind torn apart by a tragedy she could not conceive of having struck her. They guided her into the established church and there she found her pathway for a number of years. There is comfort in organised religion, there is succour in the chanting of prayers and the reassurance of the communion table. There is upliftment in the hymn singing; the coming together of like-minded people for one reason. Her confirmation marked the end of her wandering in her wilderness for some years.

But lo and behold, the pathway needed changing and once again she was thrown into the wilderness, once again finding herself virtually alone, struggling against the total collapse of all she held dear. And this time she wandered for a year before we took over, we who had been waiting for many years, guiding and pushing her into the movement in which she has found a new pathway, one that will last to the end of her natural life on this earth plane. One she had to follow, for she had been chosen to write these books for us discarnate beings and she could not have written them where she was, in the safety and security of civilisation. She had to walk her wilderness again. She had to have all barriers broken down, all secure things removed to make room for new thoughts, new ideas, new ways of doing things. But now she knows she did not walk it alone, either then or now: she knows she is held in high regard by the Realms and the knowledge, as with him who walked the earth so many years before, bolsters the most failing spirits.

She has just looked at the words on the screen and thought: lo and behold? Do angels talk like that?

Yes, we do, when we choose, when it is right. Where do you think the biblical writers got it from?

So - And lo and behold, when he walked out of the wilderness, he had changed. He had broken down many barriers. He had all secure things taken from Him. He knew he had to leave his family and go out into the world with the message which had been given to him during his time in the wilderness. He had new thoughts, new ideas, new ways of doing things which would not go well with the authorities. But God had commanded and he was there to obey. After all, was he not the Son of God?

And most of all, he knew we were with him at all times, for he saw us during those deep meditative hours. He was aware of our presence, of our love, our protection and our strength. It gave him added courage to set out on his chosen pathway, to walk out of his wilderness.

Ministry

First he went home. How simple a statement, how meaningful the words! He went home for his mother was waiting, with a new robe she had woven for him, a seamless robe of great strength and fine quality. She did not, as others might have done, start demanding "Where have you been? We were worried about you!" but greeted him calmly as if every day of the week a son walks back in after forty days in the wilderness, looking tired, weak, gaunt, lined with dirt and grime but with a new determined look in his eyes and a new set to his lips that boded no good for those around him in authority. He had bloomed, he had blossomed, he had changed despite the rigors of the time spent alone and the many battles fought out during the long hours of the cold nights.

He stayed for a while, absorbing the quiet family life around him, the hustle and bustle of the village, the coming and going of neighbours, of traders, of animals and goods but before long word came that John known as the Baptist had been arrested and he knew his time had come to truly begin work. He bade goodbye to his parents and set off on foot, alone, across the barren land, to Capernaum where he began his true ministry. There he began to call the people together and preach the message:

"Repent; for the Kingdom of Heaven is upon you!"

They came and they listened and they took his words into their hearts. He had to begin then for John, known as the Baptist, was in a cold cell, away from people, on his last journey. The work had to go on. This was his destiny, this was his pathway, this was his calling. This was the beginning of our real work.

I walked with him every step of the way but others came to help at this time, for the demands for strength and reassurance were heavy. Raphael had shared the duties of the wilderness with me, as he had throughout his life so far, but we needed more now, calling up reinforcements for the real work had begun at last.

Oh, there was exhilaration in the knowledge that we were on our way! That the waiting time was over, that the long sleepy days of Nazarene living were gone, that there were challenges ahead and much work to be done! Angels can get pretty bored hanging around with not much to do, not much work in view, not much protecting to be done … you get the picture? Of course you do.

Angels love challenges – it is a good moment to say that protecting people on the earth plane falls into two categories – challenging and downright boring. My channel gives me some hard times looking after her, she is rarely boring but others have been. She is smiling as she writes that line – that is good, it is time to get the smile back. I confess I do spend time making her smile, as does the companion she has who calls himself her Fool, for the one thing you need more than anything is laughter. I also confess that with this one, this beloved one, I can be foolish and crazy if I wish, not the serious all powerful, all knowing archangel and that in itself can be a relief for me, too. We are part human inside, you see.

Back to the story…

Imagine then, if you will, this powerful man, young, determined, forthright, taking no nonsense from anyone, arguing with the local teacher, full of knowledge and full of the power of God himself, standing up before the crowds and preaching his message of repentance and love for one another. One after the other they came, then in their tens, then in their dozens and then in their twenties and finally hundreds to listen to the new preacher in town, one who had fire in his eyes, power in his hands and oh such conviction in his heart that all who heard him believed! Power in his hands? They knew it not then, but they were to find it out soon enough. He was finding out that at times the hands tingled and he would look at them as if expecting them to have changed into something else. He did not then understand but the time for enlightenment was fast approaching. But before then…

It was time for him to find some companions, people to share the journey, to help spread the word, to take on such tasks as finding a bed for the night and food for the morning. We knew who we wanted, they had been picked out in advance, but we needed him to do the choosing, rather than us bring the men to him. It had to be his choice – if ever a human being is said to have choice and freewill, for are we not filling your heads with thoughts, impressions and directions from the time of rising through to the time of rising, taking in the sleep state along the way? But it is the look of the thing, you understand, we cannot and do not do it all. You might even rebel from time to time and not do what we want – for a while – but somehow, are your feet not back on the path again?

So we whispered in his ear as he slept one night under the tree, in the open, protected as always by a ring of angels and other heavenly beings who were there for no other reason but to guide his every footstep. We whispered of a need for companions to walk the path with him. He rose next morning with a determination to find himself some companions.

After a handful of dates and some milk, he set off along the edge of the Sea of Galilee. As I recall, it was a glorious morning, almost soft, the sun lying across the great Sea with all its glory reflected in the water. Raphael was with me that morning, he commented on the glory of it all as we walked along in his footsteps, watching everywhere and everyone as we did all the time. There were some boats drawn up at the water's edge and fishermen were mending nets and doing fishermen type things to their boats; fixing this and mending that and scrubbing things as fishermen tend to do. Mostly they think more of their boats than of their fellow man. But as he walked past, he said oh so casually, "if you come with me, I will make you fishers of men." And as if hypnotised (which we think they were at that moment) the two men dropped everything and walked away from all they held precious and dear to be with him.

"Who are you?" they asked.

"I am called Jesus," he told them. "And who are you?"

"Simon, called Peter and my brother Andrew."

"You are content to leave your possessions and come with me?"

"We are!"

"The way ahead is hard, strewn with rocks and heartache but the reward will be a place with your Lord God."

"It is enough," said Simon Peter. At that time he had no psychic powers; it is to be asked, would he have answered so had he been able to see into the future? Raphael says he doubts it very much. I say he would have gone with him no matter what, even if it had meant certain death at the end of that day for his power was tremendous even at that time. Raphael does agree with that, at least.

"Then there are two," he said, with the smile that captivated men and women alike, for it was gentle and it was warm and it was sincere and it was pure love.

"And look, there are two more! Come and join me!" he called to two younger men working on a boat with an older man. The two men looked at one another, looked at the older man and then back at him.

"We have to go, Father," said one of them and they climbed down and hurried up the slope to where he and his two new friends were standing waiting for them. One held out his hand to Jesus.

"I don't know who you are, friend, but you have a voice and mission I want to be part of. The name is James, son of Zebedee."

"And I am his brother John," said the other one, also holding out his hand.

Jesus smiled. "And then there are four. This is Simon, known as Peter and his brother Andrew. I am Jesus, late of Nazareth."

"We've heard of you!" said John, getting very excited. "You're the one who was baptised in the Jordan and who has been preaching the Word of the Lord God ever since!"

"Are you content to leave your possessions and come with me?" he asked, just to be sure.

"We are," they both said.

"And the father there, left with your boats, what does he say of your departure?"

John looked a little startled. "Why … you could not have heard us call him Father from this distance, how did you – and why-"

Jesus smiled that smile which caught at their hearts. "I know," he said gently. "If you want proof, I can tell you he said 'God be with you, dear sons, for you do his work."

The two brothers were struck dumb for a few moments for that was precisely what their father Zebedee had said to them in that moment when they decided to walk away from all they knew and cared for to go with a stranger into the unknown. And they knew more than ever that their destiny lay with this powerful wonderful man who could read minds and knew what was being said a fair distance from where he stood.

So they walked on, the five together, discussing the future, discussing the task, the spreading of the message, how they would divide the work and how they would support and work with him. Every suggestion was good and every one of them worked out in one way or another.

Not that he spoke much, he let them chatter on, getting to know one another, forming a bond of friendship and loyalty to one another as well as devotion to him, for the friendship bond would need to be strong in the future, when the tide turned as he well knew it would.

The four had heard of him and his work but had not seen him, so when they came to Capernaeum that Sabbath, they were keen for him to go to the synagogue and preach and they would sit at the back and be proud that they were his friends and associates.

The power of his teaching shook both them and the congregation but a greater shock was coming for a man possessed of a devil, one you would today confine to some quiet institution somewhere, burst out in the middle of the service, "What do you want with us, oh Holy One!"

"Silence!" he commanded. "Leave that man this instant!"

The poor afflicted man fell to the floor, writhing in agony but none went near, not even his new friends. All were afraid of the devils that might come out. In a very short time the man was looking around him with big, startled, but completely sane eyes. He struggled to his feet and looked down at himself.

"Cured," he muttered. "Cured, by the love of God!" He raised his eyes to Jesus and then fell to his knees. "Thank you, Jesus of Nazareth!"

He nodded calmly as if it was an everyday occurrence. "Take a seat, listen to the rest of the teaching, it will feed your soul." And the man sat and listened and everyone – without exception – was shocked senseless and mute by the power of this man who spoke with authority on the great teachings and who could command a devil to leave. We knew he was a healer, he hadn't known he was a healer - until that moment. Raphael and I exchanged looks and smiles. Floodgates had been opened. A new surge of power was coursing through him and he shone as if with an inner radiant light which I think only we saw but the power was such that, although the congregation could not and probably did not see it, they certainly felt it.

And in that moment the course was set for the biggest crowd drawing imaginable for word spread like wildfire that here was a preacher and a healer and a man of the people who spoke of and for the people.

People are selfish. Jesus came to them with a message of eternal life, of repentance, of living by the laws of the great God. He came with sustenance for their souls and they cried for healing for their bodies. Healing he gave in abundance, for he could not turn away any who were ill. The Gospel of Mark in your Testament tells of Jesus leaving the synagogue after healing the man possessed and finding Simon's mother-in-law ill in bed. The Gospel says he took her hand and she got up and waited on him. And how after sunset they came in their droves to sit at His feet and ask for healing.

It happened just as whoever that Gospel writer is actually said. They left the synagogue, Jesus and his new-found friends, walking through the late afternoon heat toward Simon's house where he hoped for a little sustenance and a little rest for the healing had come as a bit of a shock and he needed to get his mind around this new development. But Simon said, "My mother-in-law lies ill of a fever in her bed. Can you…" knowing what he had just seen in the synagogue which represented a miracle in his eyes. And he nodded and said, "Lead on. We will see what we can do for her," as if healing was something he did every moment of every day, instead of it just happening to him for the first time.

It took no more than his taking her hand to lift her from the bed and as she rose up, so the fever fell from her like an unwanted blanket. She was made whole in that second of rising. Her joy was unbounded for the fever had been draining her of all strength and her duties lay undone, a pain to a heart that took pride in housewifely duties. So she was pleased to wait on them all.

A simple meal was prepared, bread broken, food consumed, chatter around the table which somehow he was heading without realising he had been placed there, as if by accident and the others grouped themselves around him but lower down. He had been given His first pedestal. He had carried out his first 'miracle'. And the word was already spreading of the healing and they were gathering outside, in the cool of the evening, on crutches, on the arm of a friend or relative, in the arms of someone if they were young and helpless and in despair. They came with their many burdens and looked for easement.

"Lord, they come to see you."

We understand. It is easier to ask for easement on the earth plane than look for future easement in the hereafter, for in every human heart there lingers the tiniest of doubts that all will not be well when they make the transition to the other side, that there may not be an afterlife after all. So look for easement now - not for easement later. That being said, we also felt – my channel just erased the word resentment for I said it and I knew it was wrong even as I said it and her fingers paused, waiting for the replacement word and it never came. Instead she is typing a long explanation that seems to have strayed from the point.

Angels do not feel resentment – as such. But angels do have some human emotions for some of us were once souls upon the earth plane a very, very long time ago. We knew of jealousy, resentment, greed, anger, heartache, sorrow, grief, despair – things we have long since left behind in favour of joy, laughter, love and pure radiant happiness. Yet at that time when the sick, the lame, the feverish and the possessed came to take his healing from him, it was all I could do not to throw my great wings around him and demand of the people that they go home until they knew how to treat one such as he.

Raphael knew my feelings for he was as close to me as we both were to the one we guarded. His warning glance told me to stand back and let the people come, that it was something he had to learn to handle for it was the way it would be for the remainder of his ministry. Yes, I said to Raphael in my mind, yes, I understand but I do not like it.

We do the work of the great God, Raphael responded wisely and calmly. We obey the One greater than this one and we must do his bidding too. Nothing must cause this one to stray from the path.

So we stood back and we watched and we helped with power so that he could lay hands on each who came to kneel before him and receive the healing power. The fame was spreading, for each sick person who went away well went to tell another sick person and indeed some well people about this new man who could heal with just a touch.

And he went to bed that night with worry in his mind and turmoil in his heart. All night he tossed and turned and long before the golden fingers of dawn reached out for the land, he had wrapped himself around with a blanket and walked off to find a lonely place, there to sit in meditation and ask for guidance. He sat slumped forward under a tree, lost in a deep meditative trance and was there when his friends approached. They did not know whether they could touch him or not, afraid of the state he seemed to be in. Finally John spoke softly: "they are come looking for you once again."

Slowly he came back from his trance and looked at them with love in his eyes, knowing they had approached out of love and out of concern for his well-being.

"If they are come, then I should be there for them but then we must go, for there is a message to be preached and it will not be preached from one place."

And so he had some food and once again sat healing the sick and the disabled and the sore of heart and the possessed, most of all they seemed to bring to him those who were possessed. After the heat of the day had passed, they packed up a small amount of food into bags, shouldered these and, armed with stout walking sticks, bade goodbye to their families and began the long trek around Galilee, preaching the Word of God and healing the people wherever they went.

The Gospels say 'and from time to time he would withdraw to lonely places for prayer.'

It seemed a lonely thing to do and it was hard for his friends, now calling themselves disciples, or followers, to accept that he needed to remove himself entirely from human company to allow himself to draw into his inner being the silence, the calm, the love that comes from the Realms to all who send out their thoughts to ask for it. At those times he would ask for healing for everyone, would ask for wisdom to preach and teach and for strength to carry the message to those who needed to hear it. And he would sit in total stillness and let the power of the great God flow back into him and he would hear his father's voice in his head.

How do we know? For at these times he knew we were there and he would come out of his trance, smile, shake his head and shoulders and look up at us, standing guard over him.

"He spoke to me," he would say with utter simplicity. "I am still doing what he wants." Sometimes he would add: "thank you."

Did he see us, or did he sense us? In the Realms we spoke freely. On the earth plane we were angel and human. Although we knew him well and walked with him, we could not and would not pry into that human mind. We accepted what we could see and hear and understand of his acceptance of us being there. Whatever and wherever, he knew we were there but that was the only time he acknowledged our presence. Imagine what the people would have thought had he began speaking to what was – to them – empty air! You who are of the Spiritualist movement must understand that at that time there was no sense of such a movement. Yes, certain priests spoke certain prayers to the great Jehovah but for an individual outside in the country, sitting beneath a tree, to claim they had spoken to Jehovah and received a reply would have brought a different wrath down on their head. For the people were not of a mind to understand or appreciate such things. They had their religion, organising their lives from day to day and from morning to night and the thought of communing with a spirit in such a way would have been beyond their comprehension. Even today, the Gospel writers' words are misinterpreted by many Christian people:

'He would withdraw to lonely places for prayer.'

Prayers were for the synagogue or the precisely prescribed prayers at certain points of the day. People did not withdraw to lonely places to pray. But for him, it was a good reason to withdraw from the multitudes who dogged his every footstep and hung on his every word. It was a reason his disciples could and would understand.

Us angels were glad of the rest at times, glad when he decided to go into these lonely places, for we could stand around him with our wings out to protect the soul from whatever evil might be out there and draw some of the power of the great God into ourselves to give us strength for the time ahead, too. Doorkeepers we were, responsible for not allowing any evil entity in during these precious silent times. Doorkeepers and guardians, protectors of the soul of the man we walked with. A time for us to commune with each other, those who walked with us at this time, a time to send messages back to the Realms for those whose turn it had been or those waiting to take their turn on the earth plane. A time of peace for us, too.

Stand with our wings out? My channel looks at the sentence with disbelief, for I had said, surely, that we did not need wings and in fact they were a bit of a nuisance, especially when negotiating doorways.

Maybe, but can you think of a better way of surrounding someone with protection than to stretch out massive wings of pure light and make sure they touch one another in a huge circle of love?

Right.

I rest my case.

Again.

Was protection needed? It was. The Dark Angel had not given up his aspirations to spoil this one's earthly plan for humankind. If there was a chance of a slip up here or there, if he could be diverted from the path of love onto the path of self-gratification and power, then the plan would slip entirely and the Dark Angel would get a toehold on the earth plane that would not be shifted easily. So we were on guard especially at those times, even as we drew in the great power to bolster us, to make our lights shine even brighter, to make our task a little easier.

It helps to have a sense of humour in this job, too. It can be a bit of a serious business, this preaching and teaching and going around healing people, so if I can, I like to liven things up just a little. I know he loved to laugh and I also knew there had been little chance of laughter since the ministry began but one day I saw an example of how to make him laugh and perhaps teach others a lesson at the same time.

He had sat in a small house, with a crowd of people outside, including Pharisees, teachers, scribes and others who came to test his knowledge against their teachings, trying to trip him in knowledge of the Judaic Law. (They never did succeed in that.) Raphael had seen a small procession coming, four men carrying a bed on which lay a critically sick man. He pointed them out to me and I saw the possibility for a little fun and a lesson, as I said.

There was no way the procession would be able to get through the crowd, it was too tightly packed and no one would give way for something as large as a bed. As I said earlier, people are selfish and they were there for their own gratification, their own healing, their own answers to questions.

Ensuring he had enough guardians at that time, I slipped out of the crowd and approached the group in the guise of one of the disciples.

"You won't get through the crowd," I told them. They looked miserable, downcast and desperate. The man on the bed just looked at me weakly, not saying a word. "But I have an idea." I admired their determination and loyalty to carry the man to see him and was also interested to see what these 'stuffed full of importance' bodies would make of the demonstration.

And so I told them of my idea which lit up their faces and they gained a huge burst of energy. They found a ladder and climbed to the roof of the house, pulling the man up to the roof on his bed and then took the tiles off, one by one, laying them to one side. Then, when they had a sufficiently big hole, they lowered the bed down right in front of him.

By this time I was back by his side, waiting for his reaction. He roared with laughter which was infectious, of course, and most of those gathered there also rocked with laughter. Only the strait-laced Pharisees and teachers stood stony faced.

When the laughter dried up, he touched the man. "Your sins are forgiven," he said.

"You blaspheme," said one strait-laced Pharisee, wearing more vestments than the others, obviously more important than the others. "Only God has the power to forgive sins."

"Does not healing come from God?" he asked. They nodded, reluctantly. "Then the forgiveness of sins can also come from God via a person who gives healing." He looked at them. "You were not amused," he said. "These men carry their friend here, determined that he will be healed. They find a way, a most novel way, of getting him to me. It amused me, it amused many gathered here." He waved his hand at the crowd and they shouted their versions of 'Yes!' to the poker-faced men. "It is as easy for me to say: 'your sins are forgiven' as it is to say 'pick up your bed and walk.' Without even a touch from Jesus, the man got up from his bed, said his grateful thanks, waved to his friends and left the house. They shouted their thanks as they replaced the tiles and they too left.

I caught his eye for a moment and he did something he never did in public: He smiled at me. He knew.

Packing up, moving on, great crowds following him, waiting on his every word and his every move. Preaching, teaching, lecturing, demanding repentance and a return to the ways of God, words that could not fail to stir the hearts of all who heard him and words that could not fail to find favour with those in authority – if they were not so concerned with their own well-being and status in life.

And another of those magical moments came when he called to Levi, a tax collector, who walked away from his job to join the band of disciples.

And yet another when the centurion approached him for healing for his son. Did Jesus know then he could do distant or absent healing? Probably is the answer to the question, for as the man talked of his authority, so he stood there sending out his thoughts and yes, the boy was healed from that moment. And we who walked with him at that time looked at one another and smiled, for we knew he had discovered another gift, another aspect to his healing abilities and we knew that he would want time to consider this aspect, too.

And so it was. He made his way to a quiet place to be alone with his thoughts and his God. And we stood guard as always, wings outstretched, comforting, confining, sheltering, loving. Pouring our love into him for he needed it at that time, he was finding it very draining, all these demands on him for preaching, for healing, for companionship and leadership. It comes naturally to one such as he but only at cost, the cost of human tiredness and doubts of one's own ability. It is natural, it is human: we would not have had it any other way. We did our best in his moments of quiet to still the doubts, to instil confidence and, most of all, strength.

The Gospels say that it was the leper who was the undoing, who spread the word so far that he could no longer enter a town but had to stay in the countryside, but in truth the leper was only one small part of it. The many he healed went home to talk of the miracle they had received and more flooded to see him, hear him and be in his presence. And so he had to stay in the countryside, for the towns were not big enough to hold the crowds any more.

And so we had reinforcements flown in. Literally. During the dark hours, when the towns slept and the crowds had dispersed to their own hearths and beds, angels arrived, one by one, dropping in like fireflies, flickering lights in the darkness that, if anyone had seen, would take them for no more than a night light somewhere and go back to their sleep. He often laid awake, wondering, worrying, thinking, planning another simple parable to pass on, another simple analogy to offer to farming people who lived on and from the land and a clear message contained in it. He also thought of those who wanted to follow him but who could not or would not give up their possessions. He had nothing but his robe. But we were there, in force, a true angelic force field, around him every night and every day, walking in his footsteps, often walking before him, although he did not always know it, certainly walking alongside him, keeping the crowd back just a little.

And it was our strength that gave him the nerve, as it were, to defy the authorities.

It is forbidden for the orthodox people to do anything on the Sabbath, apart from attend the synagogue. No physical work must be done. So when the man with the palsied arm turned up at the synagogue, he thought he would take the chance to do some healing and offer the orthodox a lesson in compassion at the same time. Is healing physical work? Whatever, he challenged them and when he did not receive an answer, he told the man to hold out his arm, which was promptly restored to full health.

It aroused their ire; the beginning of the serious plotting began then, as if it had not been going on before, of course! We knew it had and we were pretty sure he knew, too. Not much got past his piercing gaze, certainly not the consciences of those who were around him. His disciples were pretty well clear in their minds but some who came to him had treachery in their hearts, for sure. Were they sent by the Dark One or were they just human beings who could not bear to see someone getting famous and getting attention? Raphael, compassionate as ever, says they were human. My view is some were sent by the Dark Angel, for he was constantly under review and under attack. At any time he could walk away from the chosen path and take the route of least resistance and the Dark One would have scored a major victory. We knew it, he knew it: we were all on guard against it.

It is hard for us to give to you the physical image of the time when he taught from the boat, for the crush of people was so great he was in danger of being pushed into the water anyway. So the boat was pushed out a little way and he sat in the bow and preached to the gathered masses. And such was the power of his voice that they were silent and absorbed every word. We can only ask that you imagine a huge crowd of people all clustered at the edge of the Sea of Galilee, surrounding Jesus and his disciples, calling, pleading, begging for healing, for words of comfort and consolation. Healing they had, for he held out his hands and all felt the great power coming from them. Words of comfort they had for he spoke with love and of love, the love for one's neighbour, for those who were in need, for those who offended, asking for forgiveness for all who had done anyone wrong.

Love. Such a difficult word for so many to comprehend.

Love. Such a difficult emotion for so many to handle.

Love. Such a powerful force in the world – then and now.

By then he had called his many disciples to him. And they had all given up their life and their possessions to walk with him.

And more reinforcements were flown in, for each disciple needed more than just their usual guardian angel at this time.

So there were additional angels to take care of –
Simon, known as Peter.
James and John, called the Sons of Thunder
(an example of his humour again)
Andrew
Philip
Bartholomew
Matthew
Thomas
James son of Alphaecus
Thaddaeus
Simon the Zealot
Judas Iscariot.

And the women, Susannah, Joanna, Rebecca, Miriam, all welcome, all made themselves useful, all contributed to the group. Don't let anyone tell you otherwise.

All these were given the gifts of healing, of 'driving out devils' (which you would know as curing mental illness) and the power of preaching, for the word had to be spread far and wide. And so the angels were dispersed to go with them, for but the shortest time there was the greatest accumulation of angel power on the earth plane that had ever been known. There was such a rustling of wings, such a shussussing of robes, (all right, as my channel stares at the word, I admit there is no such word but if you know of a real word to describe the angel robes swishing and shishing against each other, then I would be glad to know it!) such an accumulation of light and power that the very earth seemed to respond by giving up its very heart of fruitfulness, producing heavy crops such as had never been seen before, producing shoals of fish that broke nets, producing fruit on trees such as no one had ever remembered seeing before so that there was food for all.

There was healing and there was healing and there was more healing. The blind saw, the deaf heard, the palsied walked again, the possessed were restored and lepers were cleansed. The girl was brought back from the 'dead' for she was but in a very deep coma and he roused her from it and restored her to her family. And the woman in the crowd? As my channel looked at the story in Mark's Gospel, the one we have followed mostly during this book, she is remembering someone dismissing this story as nonsense. It was not nonsense. Many jostled him, many touched him just to say they had but she, the woman with the haemorrhages, touched his clothes with a purpose, to draw some of his power and it was this that made him stop and turn and ask: "who touched me?" and gave her his blessing when she came forward to admit that it was she. He had so much power in him that the merest touch of someone determined on taking some of it aroused his sensibilities and shocked his disciples who had no real understanding at that time of the depth of his powers and abilities.

Apart from those in comas, there were actual occasions when he raised people from the dead. The story of the young man restored to his mother is true. We were there. Raphael and I were there. In empathetic touch with him. We felt his grief when he saw the mother's distress. It was almost a 'here we go again, guys, hold onto your wings!' and yes, he went forward and raised the young man from his bier. And then there is the story of Lazarus – it has been said that Lazarus was never the same again, for he had looked into the Summerlands and was drawn back to this earth plane for a further period. Such a near-death experience – all right, a real death experience – is bound to change someone. That is why Lazarus was different! But I get ahead of myself – again.

I hope that those who are reading these words will not be disappointed that I have left out all the preaching, the parables, the stories to the disciples. There is no need for me to cover ground already adequately covered in every edition of the Book of Life, from the stately almost sonorous but majestic King James Version (the one my channel loves the best) through the New English Bible which she has worked with to the paraphrased Living Bible and every variation in between, every language, every interpretation, the teachings, preachings and stories are there for you to read and to understand. He spoke with simplicity and directness, there is nothing hidden in the teachings that needs a great mind to bring out. He spoke to those who had simple lives, who had not read a book or thought much about life apart from their own day to day living and regular attendance at the synagogue. His stories were direct to them, direct to their hearts, often to their consciences, too. My task is to brush away the many myths and rumours which abound when such a life is lived on this earth plane and to obviate statements such as: the miracle of the bread and fishes did not happen. How many people have tried to explain that one away! Stories such as the fact he did not die but lived on, married and had children … that one we will deal with in its appropriate place.

We have gone back, my channel and I, for she has reminded me that the death of John known as the Baptist came here, before the miracle of the loaves and fishes. We were further into the book; forgive us for the side-line, I had overlooked the sequence in my haste to reach the next part of the 'story'. This is why I am using a writer to do the work, a writer who is also an editor, for she is able to pick up the inconsistencies where angel power has surged forward and overlooked a few things.

Like the sad death of John known as the Baptist. Done out of spite and jealousy, done because of the whim of a human, not knowing that they did the will of the Godhead, for it was right that the prophet should go home then.

At this time John known as the Baptist was in his prison cell, hearing of the great deeds outside. But, human as he was, he had his doubts, so he asked his disciples to go to the Nazarene and ask; "are you the one who is to come, or are we to expect some other?"

In front of them he reached out and healed the sick, the blind, the disabled, the possessed and said to them: 'go tell John what you have seen, how the sick are healed and the dead brought back to life and the poor given the good news.' And so every prophesy that was ever made regarding the coming of the Messiah was being fulfilled through these two great men, although none knew it at the time.

I have learned since that time that John known as the Baptist was one very frustrated soul. Just when he thought he should be out, preaching his message of repentance, he was shut behind stone walls, unable to reach the people he so longed to serve. The Wild Man was a man of compassion, of great love and wisdom, of strength and character. He also longed to see for himself what miracles were taking place, what healing was going on round the Sea of Galilee and across Judaea, what was being said by the man everyone talked of. And so he paced his prison cell and cursed and raged at the authorities who locked him away.

But this too was part of his progression, for his part in the story of Jesus of Nazareth was all but over. He had done his task well, brought the people to hear the message of repentance, baptised the man himself in the Jordan and heard the voice of God. His role was over. His time was almost over, too, but as I have said already, this soul has been back time and time again to take up causes, defend the weak and the unjustly persecuted, often dying young only to reincarnate and start over again.

Yes, he is here now. Yes, he is working against injustice. No, I can't tell you where he is or who he is. But look for the lone fighter, the voice in the wilderness, the one standing up against inhuman acts. Consider the life of Martin Luther King and ask yourself … and there have been many, many others. Your world would be a poorer place were it not for fighting souls like the one you know as John known as the Baptist.

He wanted to grieve in the quietness of his mind when the news was brought to him and he tried to find a quiet place with His disciples but the crowd followed. And went on following for two days.

The loaves and fishes. It is impossible, they say, for so few loaves and fishes to feed five thousand people.

So, they say, obviously everyone had food with them and they all shared and everyone ate and there were twelve baskets of scraps left over.

I say – it is impossible for someone suffering from incurable cancer to be cured.

I say – it is impossible for someone who could not walk to be able to walk.

I say – it is impossible for someone who was deaf to hear again.

I say – it is impossible for someone who was blind to see again.

I say – it is impossible for someone with severe mental illness to be cured.

I say – it impossible for a leper to be cured with just a touch.

Now you say, but these things happened then and happen today, through absent and hands-on healing.

I say – if you believe the healing, then believe the story of the bread and fish. I do not think he intended a miracle, as such. I believe, and remember I was standing right by his side when the boy came with the simple meal, that when he saw how small the offering of food was against the great crowd, nearer the thousand than five thousand, by the way! His heart was stirred with compassion to a degree that he was able to take the food and hand it out and hand it out and hand it out … and in a moment, small fires were lit and the fish was cooked and the bones were gathered up and yes, it filled twelve baskets which were then taken and thrown into the sea to feed the fish so that the bounty of the sea could be drawn on yet again.

And when he sat and looked at the small loaf he held and the small fish he held and saw that everyone was able to eat, including his new friends and companions, then he held up the food and offered it as a blessing to them all. And he ate of His own bountiful goodness and love for all those who had devotedly followed him, the men, the women, the children who could not get enough of his preaching and his presence.

And he turned and looked at me and I think he knew then that he had done something he shouldn't, perhaps, for healing is one thing but the feeding of a multitude is another and it was noted, documented, stored against him in the file marked "Troublemaker." Raphael came over to me and said – mind to mind – 'a major miracle, what will they make of that back in Jerusalem?' and we both knew it would count against him although those who were fed were filled with gratitude for the sustenance he had given them out of the goodness of his heart.

Miracles. What are they? A change in the natural laws which govern this earth plane? Something for which there is no rational explanation? Your scientists are hard to put to prove eternal life yet it has been proved time and time again. They cannot prove telepathy but it is there, it is a fact. They cannot prove spiritual healing but stand back in amazement and shock when the incurable are cured. Love cannot be proved but its power transcends anything this earth plane has to offer.

It is a miracle that you are on the earth plane at all. A miracle that day after day you live, breathe, think, rationalise, feel. A miracle that you experience all the emotions that there are to be experienced, that you weep, laugh, cry, smile, every one of you. A miracle that the sun comes up and gives warmth and light to your planet. Imagine the vastness of that miracle and know that the so-called 'feeding of the five thousand' was indeed a small miracle although it had a great impact at the time. Accept the miracles he caused to happen and be glad they did happen and perhaps sorrow a little that you were not there to see them, for such things have not been seen since nor will they be, for none walk this earth plane as he did and none bring the degree and intensity of love that he did. Those great miracle workers you have had have proved to be oh so human, with faults that have sullied their reputations and their miracle workings. Those who used the power of their minds to control others were paid back with desolation and despair at the end. Those who used the power of their mind to elevate others, such as the Buddha, Gandhi, Mother Teresa and people like that were – or will be - elevated to sainthood for the work they did for humanity out of love for humanity. The Buddha and others never created miracles; they simply gave out love and direction for humanity to follow and as such were true followers and servants of the great white spirit of love.

Apologies to my readers for the lecture; I felt it had to be said. Many have decried the miracles he did, finding 'logical' explanations for them, or dismissing them out of hand as mere illusions or tricks played by himself and his disciples on the gullible. My words remain the same. Accept them for what they were; an outpouring of love for all who came to him, whether their need was physical or mental. He gave them food. He gave them healing. He gave them thought and guidance for their spiritual development, to enrich their souls. He gave them hope. He gave them love.

And this was why they followed him in such vast crowds. No trickster could keep such a crowd with them, no fraudster could continually defraud an entire population – or so it felt at times.

And because of the crush, the heat, the demands, the power they drained from him, He continued to make his way to the lonely places to commune with the Godhead. And then we were able to come close to him, to shield the fragile soul from the multitude, to keep all evil and would-be evil from his vicinity. For those who would see him fall were close at all times, watching his every word, his every movement, his every healing and his every miracle. And the resentment grew large among the Pharisees, scribes and lawyers who sought to catch him out on the law or on clerical grounds. Every time he had an answer for them and they had to back off, confounded and dumb-founded and amazed that someone from the little known town of Nazareth should have such knowledge, such power, such skill at teaching the people.

But when he returned to his home town to preach they did not want to know or hear him. No one can be a prophet in their own town, for everyone knows you and has an opinion on you and find it hard to take you seriously. So he went away and spoke to others in other towns, other areas, bringing his message of repentance, of love, of neighbourly duty and sacrifice. And the more he spoke, the more the people came and the more the authorities schemed and planned and deceitfully worked to bring him down.

For what reason? He made no challenge to their authority; he did not seek to take their income from them.

So – what was at the root of it?

Ego.

He drew bigger crowds than anyone around. He spoke with authority that the most learned of them could not inject into their voice. He had a way with simple stories, parables, teachings and prayers that touched the hearts of many. You recite these prayers even today and study his Sermon on the Mount, do you not? What do you know of the Pharisees and Scribes of that time?

Precisely.

I rest my case.

Hmmm. Anyone would think at some time in my incarnations I had been a lawyer! Who knows … my incarnations are something I am not telling the world – the people who need to know already know and that is sufficient for now. Sorry…

My channel has just turned the page of Luke's Gospel and seen the story of the woman living an immoral life who came to the house of the Pharisee and there bathed his feet with her tears and anointed his head with oil. This is a story made much of over the many years since it happened – and it happened! Once again it was an act done in pure love and adoration for what he was and it gave him a chance to give one of his lectures again, driving the message home of forgiveness of sins, of living in peace, of being of a quiet mind, which is what it all came down to in the end. It was a love story in miniature. As I recall it, she never spoke a word. It was all done without the need for words, just the anointing, the tears and her hair to wipe it all away. And he was as deeply moved by it as we were. Such love for such a man! Would that the rest of the world saw him in the same light!

Quite a big crowd were now out doing the preaching rounds, as we thought of it. There were the twelve disciples and the women who had joined the group, some who had been cured of various illnesses and those attracted by his aura of power and magnetism. Fortunately for them, the women bought and prepared the food, or they would have gone very hungry at times.

And yes, it is true, his long suffering mother saw very little of him during this time. If she tried to visit, the crowds were such that she could not get near her son, whose reputation was spreading so fast there was nowhere he could go to escape, to be free. It made no difference to her love, for the love of a mother is greater than anything else on earth. She was proud but worried, bursting with admiration for all he had achieved and scared sick inside of the end result. For she knew, as well as anyone, the vindictiveness of the men of the temple who saw a threat to their way of life.

During this time, during what we thought of as the preaching rounds, Jesus developed full clairvoyant abilities. It came upon him slowly, so that he was not fully aware at times that he was giving messages, as it were, but he had the gift. So it was when a rich man approached him and asked for the way to Heaven, he was able to pinpoint with absolute accuracy the man's love for his wealth. When he met the woman at the well, he knew immediately about her past, her many husbands, her way of living and told her so. Only a clairvoyant could have known such things and said such things with such certainty. There are many instances recorded in the Gospels of the times he was able to speak directly to people, as if reading their very hearts. Remember the classic time when they tried to catch him out on rendering tributes to Caesar, how he read their intention clearly, showed them a coin and said 'Render under Caesar that which is his and unto God that which is His.' And totally confounded their argument with simple logic. But logic made to look simple through knowledge, through clairvoyance, through being able to 'read' their intentions.

And did he quell the storm? Well … with a little angelic help, yes, he did. You see, we could not let the plan go because of a boat going down in the Sea of Galilee and it gave the disciples something to think about. Has this not happened many times? Something happens, a crash, a disaster of some kind and people walk away from it unhurt, unmarked and intact? In a landslide/earthquake in South America, an entire village of 1500 people was wiped out. But a child survived. Why? Because he has a mission, a path to follow and his angelic guardians made sure he was kept safe, while everyone else perished and everything he knew was taken away. Hard lessons but remember, he chose that before he came. Oh yes, that teaching is oh so true! Think on the many instances where many have perished but a few have survived. And ask yourself why. And remember the answer we have given – that they have a path to follow and their angelic guardians made sure they followed their path by ensuring they survived.

So we were there to help quell the storm and quieten the waves and give the disciples a new thing to worry about. For they had become a little complacent, a little too accepting, a little too demanding for themselves, who would be the greater, silly arguments like that. They needed shaking up rather radically. It seemed a good way of doing it. A sort of practical joke, if you want to think of it that way but with a serious intention behind it.

It worked. They stood in total awe of him who had the power and they stopped their bickering – for a few days at least.

He stepped from the boat and was met by a 'madman' besieged with many devils. He was cured, of course, it became second nature to him now to reach out to the sick and possessed and heal them, but it scared the living breath out of those who saw it, those who were watching over the herd of swine. The animals panicked and went over the cliff, giving rise to the story that the devils went into them. Instead of impressing them, he had terrified the local community and they asked him, oh so politely, to leave.

So He did but with much sadness for there was work to be done there, words to be spread, healing to be carried out but when you are not wanted, the best thing to do is beat a hasty retreat. This they did, getting back in the boat and setting sail for their homeland again. They left behind one sane man, cured of his 'possession' and with a story to tell which he spread far and wide, so the word went out anyway. Seeds, always the seeds, planted and nurtured in the right place at the right time.

The journey back was uneventful, by the way…

My channel has just scrolled back (her terminology) through the book to find the point where I mentioned the woman touching his robe. According to Luke's Gospel, this event came after the boat trip, she is thinking. I am saying, does it matter? I mentioned that earlier in a section about his healing, so – be sure most of the major miracles are covered somewhere, some way, somehow in this narrative. It's not so much a biography as a sort of narration of a life, so it might just skip around a bit, here and there … the essence of it is my observations. And after all, who are these Gospel writers but latter day scribes, are you sure they got it in the right order? My channel tells me I would have made a good lawyer …

Stay with me, it gets more interesting…

Healing Ministry

Luke says the Twelve went out preaching the good news and healing the sick.

Today in your world healers need certificates, insurance, all sorts of bits of paper and accreditation before they can put their hands on or near someone. Then it was much simpler. Then you just put your hands on someone and you acted as a channel and the healing came through and people were cured. Simple. Effective. Difficult to carry certificates when you have no possessions and are relying on charity for board and lodging. Difficult to get insurance companies to give you cover when you have No Fixed Abode and no steady income, either.

But oh! The healing was more direct, more powerful, more instant than that going down these modern days! For they had no encumbrances, they had no distractions, they preached the good news and they healed. What joy they had in that simple task at that simple time!

Luke says 'one day he was praying alone in the presence of his disciples' which means in effect he was in deep meditation and they were there to protect him. He had a clear clairvoyant day so he said to them; 'who do the people say I am?' They said: 'some say John known as the Baptist, others Elijah, others that one of the old prophets had come back to life.' (I ask myself, what is Elijah if not one of the old prophets but there you go … maybe angels see things differently from humans…) and Jesus asked them who they thought he was.

Peter opened his mouth, as he had a habit of doing, and said "God's Messiah.' And then in his clairvoyant state, he said to them 'don't tell anyone what was just said. But remember this: there is much suffering ahead for me, I will be rejected and put to death but I will rise again.'

Before they could protest and argue and demand to know what it was all about and how he knew, he launched into a lecture on leaving self behind, taking up a cross and following him. Leaving self behind. That's a tough one for just about anyone. It takes a lot of willpower, a lot of soul searching and a lot of heartache for some people. That's why we often put them through 'a walk in the wilderness', it clears the mind beautifully and focuses life on the things which really matter. Give someone a near death experience and they will fully appreciate life and what they have. Give someone the experience of bankruptcy and in future they will appreciate the money they have. Give someone ill health and they will grow to appreciate good health when it is theirs again. Give someone a bad relationship and they will cherish a good one when it arrives. The analogy is in the animals you 'rescue' from brutal owners. They are so grateful to be loved and cared for they give more love in return than they would normally do.

So it was with those he chose and those he spoke to about leaving it all behind and following him. So it was with those who since that time have chosen their own wildernesses to walk in and have come out pure and clean and filled with Spirit, in whatever form and whatever name you care to put on it. So it is with those who walk their wilderness in your modern world and find it hard to come to terms with it all. Some don't. The autistic child does not have it in them to face the world. Those with mental illness are ones who cannot come to terms with the world, who retreat into paranoia and delusion and illusion to escape the realities of life. They are to be cared for, compassionately, for there but for the grace of spirit go we all. And let's be honest, this world of yours is a tough place to live in at the very best of times and now is not the very best of times. We know: we have walked it many times with one or other of you! Often unknown, invariably unseen, generally un-noticed and ignored. Equally often, recognised, accepted, leaned on, cared for. The one balances out the other – eventually. One day you will appreciate just how vast the love of an angel really is…

What I should have said, what I prompted my channel to write notes about this morning before the busyness of the day got between us, is that the time of which I now write is some three years after he first set out on His ministry. This fact is often overlooked by those who study the many times written and translated Gospels. We have covered many miles, back and forth around the area: Galilee, Judaea, round small villages with names you would not know, around towns whose names have become famous through His visiting them. Three years of tramping the dusty highways and byways, preaching, healing, teaching.

And this is leading to – well, one thing that does get mentioned an awful lot – are the portraits you have of him anywhere near what he really looked like? Does the psychic portrait in some of your churches accurately represent him? What of the injunction that men at that time had short hair?

I ask you first, if you are an itinerant preacher, do you have time or money for haircuts?

I ask you second, do you accept the psychic portraits given to you at meetings of light?

And I say to you, yes, his hair grew long because he had no time or money for haircuts and no real concern about how he looked anyway, the message being everything.

And I also say that the psychic portrait is as accurate as you are going to get it without seeing him for yourself. He has a calm face, a gentle smile that illuminates that face, He has piercing yet loving eyes and a mouth that is as ready to smile as it is to open and dispense yet more words of wisdom.

Accept. Don't question. The image of Jesus of Nazareth is as abiding as the legends about the man himself. It is not for man to question the man, his life, his mission or his death, although man has taken it upon himself to do so. He tries to dissect the life which was lived, but you cannot do that, for you were not there. The Gospel writers were narrators, collecting tales from witnesses, from their own recollections, some of it was divinely inspired, some was their own knowledge. And in the originals, they carried a good deal of truth. In the translations some of that truth has been lost but, fortunately for humankind, enough of his message still exists to allow you to appreciate the depth of his wisdom, his love and his humanity.

Accept. Don't question. He came, he lived, he taught, preached and healed. If in the translations some of the prayers have been changed a little, the essence of them is still there and you use it as naturally as breathing, do you not? And does not every person use the similes he gave in the parables? The sower and his seed, the Good Samaritan, the good Shepherd, the Prodigal Son, yes, familiar, welcoming, comforting, as ancient nursery rhymes are to a child. You know them; you know of them, you know then that they were divinely given for only that which endures comes from Spirit.

About this time he withdrew into the mountains for meditation and silent contemplation. He took some of the disciples with him, for they too had to learn about meditation and contemplation and the stilling of the mind for the words of Spirit to come through into the subconscious and then the conscious mind. Whilst on the mountain the disciples experienced their first transfiguration, when they saw three figures appear on the mountain top and saw that he conversed with them. We were there, we were guarding, for that moment could be dangerous for the one channelling the spirit persons. We felt the power he radiated at that time and were almost scorched by it ourselves. I know Raphael and Michael stood back a bit, afraid of wings being damaged by the sheer force coming from him. And he channelled Elijah and Moses that afternoon, there on a lonely empty mountain. They gave him good advice, sensible advice that he knew he had to follow to get through the days ahead. Time was fast running out and he knew it. The disciples weren't really listening to what was being said, they were more in awe of what was going on than paying attention, which is why we had the classic offer from Peter to build the shelters in their honour, but instead were blasted by the voice filling their minds; "This is my son, my beloved, listen to him!"

We heard it, too, being close enough to feel the vibrations and pick up the communication and I think we were as knocked out as the poor earthly beings who didn't know what to make of their experiences that afternoon. Transfiguration, disembodied voices and then, as if that was not enough, Jesus telling them not to say a word until he had risen from the dead.

First there was the word 'dead' to cope with, then the word 'risen' on top of what they had just seen and heard. Poor bewildered people, stumbling down the mountain track after him, who walked as if he had lived in such conditions all his life, finding every foothold, finding the path with an ease that amazed and baffled them as much as the things they had just seen. Reaching out for a handful of berries here, a sweet growing wild flower there, he was at the base of the mountain and back among the multitude waiting for him long before the others stumbled their weary way onto flat ground again.

Almost immediately he was caught up in controversy again, presented with the sick boy who could not be healed by his followers.

Perhaps buoyed up by what he had just experienced, perhaps really genuinely angry with those whose faith was not strong enough to heal, whatever the reason, we had an uncharacteristically snappy Jesus:

Matthew's Gospel: What an unbelieving and perverse generation! How long shall I be with you? How much longer must I endure you?

Mark's Gospel: What an unbelieving and perverse generation! How long shall I be with you? How long must I endure you?

Luke's Gospel: What an unbelieving and perverse generation! How long shall I be with you and endure you all?

Ask yourselves, how many times in the book of life do the Gospels actually relate the same incident virtually word for word? It made a bit of an impact, that outburst, but it was overdue for the disciples were not doing their job properly. They continued to hold a tiny seed of doubt that what they were doing would work. So it didn't, but it should have done. For when he commanded, the boy was healed.

Let me say here that not all healing works all the time. By that I mean that people are not cured of whatever condition they are suffering from immediately and every time. Some are. Some walk away from healing with their body and their faith intact. Others need time for the body to adjust to its new healed status, rather like losing the plaster after you break a leg, you still walk as if it was there for a while. Some will not be healed for, like it or not, it is their time to go home. What the healing does is ease the passing.

My channel once asked the question: what happens to the people who are not knowledgeable about this great force called Spirit, those who go through life never knowing they could go for healing, because in her mind it seems unfair. She hears of cancer, of heart conditions, of breathing conditions and wants to reach out to them all. This is the healer in her.

You ask for healing for all sick and suffering around the world. You do not know, you cannot know, where those prayers are targeted, how they are conveyed. Spirit knows whom it wishes to heal and whom it wishes to take home for their time is done. So, your group may pray for healing to go out around the world and Spirit may take that request and those who have work to do, in whatever field, will be cured of whatever it is that afflicts them. The others will be taken gently home. So the prayers are not wasted, not for a moment. What you do not know is that they work, for there are no letters to be published in healing magazines, no reports in newspapers of 'miracle' cures. Just people here there and everywhere around the world who get up from their sick bed and walk again. He healed all who came to him for a very good reason, it made people come to him. What you do, in your healing sessions and healing evenings, is heal the soul, the mind, the emotions of those who come to you. You may not effect a 'miracle' cure every time but people will walk away feeling better because of what you have done.

Healers of the world, unite! The world needs you, your hands, your talents, your prayers!

Back to our story. At this time there was a great weight of blackness on his heart and mind for he was heading toward the final days. It is standard practice these days to tell people you cannot and will not know the date of your passing and so it was with this soul, too, in the beginning. But he knew more than many and knew that in Jerusalem they were waiting for him with tricks, traps and all manner of deception to end his life. They did not like the words he spoke, they did not like the way he interpreted their laws and threw them back at the Pharisees, scribes and lawyers. He was a troublemaker in their eyes and troublemakers had to be done away with before they unbalanced the seat of power.

And so this young man, full of the vigour of life, full of strength and determination, full of love and hard-won knowledge, gained through hours of deep meditation and growth, knew that for him the end was indeed nigh. For him there would be no future, no wife, no children, no standing in the community and being honoured by being asked to take the Sabbath prayers. No one looking up to him, only the thousands who flocked to hear his words but for the most part they came for their own reasons. Everyone has an agenda and they had more than most: a chance to be healed, a chance to be in on what might turn out to be a popular uprising, a chance to be part of a huge media event, to hear preaching such as had never been heard before, a chance to be away from work on the grounds that a new preacher was there and you had to listen to save your soul.

In his heart at that time there was nothing but sorrow. There was so much work to be done, so much depended on him choosing the right people and sowing seeds everywhere, the seeds that would grow into a movement that would sweep the land. We drew closer to him than we had ever done; trying to support him during those last weeks before the world fell apart. He nominated yet more disciples and taught them what to do, sent them out to heal and to preach and went right on preaching and teaching and doing healing himself as well. So many stories he told, so many parables for you to live by still, two thousand years after all this happened! It was such an important time, a time when so much had to be crammed into every waking hour. He took little time out then for his meditations and silences, he worked on, trying to gather the right people and ensure they carried on the work he had begun. And he grew a little haggard and thin, as if it was all getting too much for him physically, although we knew mentally he was strong enough to carry on – for a while, at least.

Jerusalem beckoned, Jews and Romans alike waiting to 'welcome' this upstart preacher. How would you feel, walking into that kind of lion's den? Would you not turn tail and run back to Nazareth, bury yourself in a carpenter's shop, knee deep in shavings and dust, making stools, beds and other items for the locals? Would you not think the wilderness was preferable to walking into a nest of vipers all waiting to bite? Understand then that under the sermonising, the lectures to the disciples, the harassment of Pharisees and tax collectors, lawyers and those who tried to join him but who wanted to say goodbye to this one or bury their dead or sell their land before they did so and even the disciples themselves, arguing about who would sit on his right hand, there seethed a well of pure desperation, determination and sadness all churned up into a mess so devastating it was a wonder he kept going. If he had not had angelic help, he would surely not have been able to go through with it.

So he spoke his fears and future aloud to his disciples, to ensure they understood what was going to happen.

"I'm going to Jerusalem," he said. "There I'll be handed over to the foreign powers, those in command; I'll be mocked, maltreated and spat upon. Then I'll be flogged and put to death. This is what will happen. This is what I foresee. But I will rise again from the dead."

But they didn't understand. Not for a single moment could they believe that he would be so treated. This was a man they had followed around the countryside, had watched the miracles take place in front of their eyes, had learned for themselves the power of healing by touch, had seen the power of healing by thought over distance, had cast out their own devils and stood tall among the community. The thought that it would all fall around their ears was too much to take in so they shrugged their shoulders, decided it was a load of nonsense and walked on.

We know the true meaning of it all was hidden from them, as it states in the Gospels, for one very good reason. Had they believed him at that time, every last one would have turned tail and ran straight back to their homes, buried their heads in the sand and said "who?" Well, wouldn't you?

But he knew he had to go. And, being himself as he was, he decided to go in style. So he directed a few disciples to go and find the unbroken colt tethered to a tree.

"What if someone stops us?" they asked, a natural question, after all, it isn't every day you can go and take someone's animal without being accosted, is it?

"Tell them the Master has need of it," he told them.

Question. How did he know the colt would be there, how did he know he could ride it, how did he know that someone would be satisfied with that explanation for the 'stealing' of the animal?

I often wonder why scholars try to dissect the Gospels, turning them over, trying to find holes in the miracles and the teachings, but overlook these basic questions! At least, I have never seen anyone comment on them. Perhaps I don't read the right books…

If you have been perceptive enough to ask these questions, here are the answers.

He knew the colt was there through clairvoyance. He knew he could ride it for he had power over animals. He knew that someone would be satisfied with that explanation for we had visited the owner in sleep state and told him that the Messiah (or an equivalent word, enough to arouse his curiosity) would need the loan of his animal but that we would arrange to return it. So, when these two rather rough looking characters turned up, he was a bit apprehensive until he heard the code words, after which he was happy for them to take it away.

Simon Peter threw a cloak over the animal's back for him to sit on, others actually laid their cloaks on the ground for him to walk the animal over, but they gave that up after a while, it took too long to pick them up and run round and lay them down again. So they took to shouting hosannas and other great expressions of delight and love to the world. And he rode in silence, watching the crowds, his disciples, the shimmering morning heat lighting up the countryside and the great city they were heading towards. The city that would see his death and whatever was to come afterwards. Before then, he knew he was riding straight into danger. For there were the treacherous ones, the dangerous ones, the singular ones who saw only a threat to their way of life.

It was a glorious day when he rode toward Jerusalem. It was a day heavy with sadness. Raphael and I knew what was ahead, knew that time was running out, knew that we had a lot of work to do in the days to come and neither of us looked forward to the demands to be made on us or on him. We had the advantage of being 'celestial' whilst he was still human and that did help us a bit to keep our strength of mind and resolve going while he battled with his own mind on the torments ahead.

For little by little the future had opened up to him in its entirety. He knew, had known for some time, that his life span was now short. He had known that there was no chance of a commitment of marriage with anyone, that there would not be much life left to look forward to, but the actuality of the passing was now being revealed to him a little at a time. It is one thing to know you are going to die, it is quite another to know how you are going to die. Yes, he knew he would be handed over to the authorities, expected to be reviled and spat upon, expected the flogging, that was all par for the course, that was the way the Roman rulers did things. He knew he would die. John known as the Baptist was cleanly beheaded. He had in his heart hoped for a quick end, a merciful end, but that was to be denied him and that was what was slowly being revealed. The last act would be a long drawn out and painful one – for a reason he could not then appreciate.

Symbolism is everything. People cling to symbols, they use them, they are like passwords, they are useful for the illiterate, they are useful for covert and secretive organisations and gatherings. They are as potent as a flag to gather people together for one common cause. He had to create a symbol. To do that he had to die in a particularly ghastly way.

And still he rode into Jerusalem when I tell you, any sensible person would have turned that animal around and gone back to where it came from, said "thanks for the loan, I'm staying here."

Such was the power of his commitment to his chosen path that he rode into that everlastingly damned city!

Final Days

In case you were wondering, someone took the colt back to its owner and said thank you very much, the Lord appreciated the loan, rescued Simon Peter's cloak and went back to Jerusalem the hard way, on foot. Meantime the thorn in the side of the authorities was busy with his first outrage.

He remembered his first visit to the Temple when he was a small boy. Remembered how grand it was, how imposing, how awe inspiring the great sweeping soaring roofs were and how the whole place was redolent of the service and worship of God.

He walked into a market.

Money changers shouted their exchange rates, vendors with doves, goats and lambs shouted their prices, there was haggling going on, the bleating of the animals, the noise of the caged birds – it was to him an outrage. He reacted as we expected he would and did nothing to stop him for these people had to learn that a fireball had arrived in town. So he overturned the tables, set free the birds and animals, sent the people scurrying away from His blazing anger. "It is written!" he thundered, "that my house shall be a house of prayer but you have made it a robber's cave!"

Imagine what that did for his standing in the community! The people loved it; the authorities hated it. So they schemed and planned together to do away with him - but with care, for the people were coming to hear his words every bit as much as they did in the wilds of Galilee, away from 'civilisation', away from the city walls. For they had not heard such preaching with such clarity, such precise detail yet said in a way that every person could understand it and identify with everything he said. This gave those in authority a bit of a headache, to put it mildly.

So the space once occupied by tables and cages, the clink of money and the sound of doomed animals was taken up with the sound of preaching, of thanks given when healed and the sound of a doomed man.

We stopped there, my channel and I, for we both looked at the words which had appeared on the screen and paused to think about them. For her, it was a prophesy fulfilled, knowing the story in advance makes it easier to accept what happened after that. For us, at that time, it was a sense of desolation, for although we too knew what was to happen, when you have walked closely with one soul in that way, shared the trials and tribulations, guarded him in His time of silence and meditation, watched over him as he taught and healed, walked alongside him as he and Judas shared the long lonely nights talking through Judas' role in his forthcoming demise, to see it coming to its sad end struck deep chords of desolation and sadness in us.

But – if we thought there had been a conflagration of angel power when the ministry was in full flow, it was nothing to what was happening right at that time. The Realms were actually decimated, seriously short of angel power for the few days after he entered Jerusalem. This was because the final part had to be played out in all its glory and gory details and, to do that, we were all entrusted with the task of ensuring that it did in fact go according to plan. Judas' angel had to make sure he did not back out of what he had to do. The rest of the angelic force had to ensure that every person played their part. The stage was set for a violent confrontation with the authorities, Roman and Jewish, with self-seeking officials and high-ranking rabbis who wished to see an end to this troublemaker who stirred the people up in their city. So every disciple - and by then there were many of them - was guarded by angels and the main disciples, the Twelve, were double guarded whilst he had a whole phalanx of angel power around him. At times he appeared to shimmer, there was so much power around his body at that time. And he knew it and leaned on it for he needed all the strength he could get to endure the days ahead.

Can anyone really know what it is like to live out your last days? Does anyone know how a murderer on Death Row or anywhere else really feels as every day brings you nearer to the day when there will be no more days? Every meal you eat takes you closer to the last one. Every look at the sky takes you nearer to the day when your look will be the last one. Can any of us appreciate the trauma, the tension, the sheer desolation and sadness of the countdown to death?

But he acted as if every day was a good day, filled with teaching and healing and talking to the people who came to him and catching out the Pharisees in their tricks to try and trap him. You cannot trap a clairvoyant when s/he is working well and at that time he was working well.

So when the famous incident of the woman caught in adultery was brought to him and he was told the penalty was death by stoning, he turned it back on them. With hearts full of vicious intent, they stood there and asked for his opinion on the law of Moses. His answer, considered after he wrote on the ground was 'He who is without sin shall cast the first stone.' And they all left.

Death by stoning is particularly nasty. It goes on for what feels like forever. The first stone hurts, the second even more, others break bones, open veins, the pain is endless and the dying a long time in coming. It is a chance for all who have vicious thoughts to take up stones in the name of righteousness and throw them with all their strength.

And today, on your TV screens, you see an ancient people throwing stones.

Ah, this is a side-line my channel did not expect! She in fact asked what Jesus wrote on the ground; that is something we will return to in a moment. My mind is on death by stoning for it is a feared and fearsome thing to endure and to see. The people of that time were savage indeed, almost wicked in their ways of dealing out penalties for offences against the law, both canon and earth law, as it were. But emotions run high when there are morals at stake, no matter that the marriage might have been seriously bad, that the woman might have found a few hours of peace and happiness in the arms of another. Even today, adultery is whispered about, gossiped about, laughed over behind closed doors, it is still the subject of much discussion and many broken relationships. In those times, the savage uncivilised times of which we are writing, it was bodies which were broken under the hail of stones which cut, bruised, broke and finally killed.

Why am I labouring this point? There are some who have said that Jesus was not crucified, that he was not executed in that way, that the Romans did not use it as a form of execution. They are wrong. The Romans executed a lot of people that way. It was a favourite way, for they were on display as a warning and a deterrent to others. Romans staged the savage Games in the Coliseum, when animals and people were pitted against each other to fight to the death. And the spectators cheered and jeered and watched as brave men and even braver animals who had no weapons but their claws and teeth, were relentlessly killed.

But was it only the Romans who were vicious and wicked and cruel at that time? It would seem not, for many would happily stone to death a young woman who found happiness for a short time in the arms of another. These were Jews. These were not proud Romans who were busy conquering yet another land, but the people who said they were the Chosen Ones of God. Such cruelty they had then! Is it any wonder that the land they occupy now is still drenched in blood, the blood of the children, the young men, the fighters – two people fight for the same land: one side fights with modern weapons, the other reaches for the oldest weapon around – a stone.

I am not condemning! I am not saying the Jewish people are wrong, I am just saying, look at all who were there at that time and the acts they carried out.

Believe me when I say that time was blood drenched every single day in some way or another. The sadness is that it goes on today, not only in that ancient land but others, all around this world, in this so-called civilised word. There are still stonings, there are still deaths, there are still mutilations and suffering. There are those who would live by Sharia law and condemn all others who do not, without a shred of compassion or forgiveness in their hearts. God forgives, why cannot they? We see the young women killed by their relatives for the sake of 'honour' and we cry, be compassionate! Be forgiving! Remember his words at this time! Are you so righteous you can cast the first stone? We cannot see an end to it until man decides to put an end to it.

We will reach the sad part of this story before long and all will be revealed to answer the many who question, who doubt, who are distinctly sceptical of the truth of that happening.

Back to the question my channel asked: what did he write on the ground and why did he do it anyway?

He did it to give himself a few moments in which to contemplate the right answer to give. He did it because he sought an answer which we gave. He wrote 'save her?' and Raphael erased it and wrote 'yes.' He gave them their answer and then he wrote again 'right?' and we answered again 'yes.' And when he looked up, he was alone with the young woman.

Did anyone see the communication? No. If they had, the words would have been inscribed in the Gospels, but they stood back and waited to see how he would handle this latest test. What they thought of the writing on the ground no one knows. I haven't asked their angels, for this is not their story. When they write their story, then their angel will be able to supply the answer. That's if they ever do want to write their story. Some of them will not want to, for it will reveal too many human weaknesses for their liking!

A moment of indecision? Perhaps. It was the first time he had actually asked us for our opinion on something of momentous importance to his ministry. It was the first time he had been a little unsure and I believe that was because it was one of the trickiest situations he had found himself in. Oh, they had tried with so many questions and situations to catch him out in sacrilege or outright blasphemy and each time he had found the right words and confounded them.

But this situation was different. Here was a person caught out in direct breach of the Law of Moses. There was one penalty, death by stoning. Doubtless she had confessed, so there was no question of her guilt. How then to answer them without giving anything away?

So for the first time in his ministry, he sought angelic help and found the right words because we said she should be saved. That was the dilemma. Should he try and save her or allow the law to take its normal course? Once he knew He had to save her, then the right words came.

I have questions now. I have to ask why this particular episode is relegated to the end of the Gospels, why it is not an integral part of the story. Why in the New Testament my channel is using does it say 'some manuscripts here insert the passage printed on page 239' where this story is to be found? SOME manuscripts? It was a profound and quite extraordinary happening, the heights of diplomacy and almost Solomon-like in its finely balanced reasoning. And it is relegated to a passage printed on a page at the end of the Gospels! There is no rhyme or reason to the translators who worked on these writings, is there?

I choose to place it here, in an important place in this story, for you to understand and appreciate the skills he used in dealing with these Pharisees who tried so hard to trap and trick the one who was there to teach.

In the Gospels it says that he spent His days in the city and his nights on the hill called Olivet. Yes, he slept rough. Yes, they all tried to find a place on the grass where they would be comfortable and pulled rough blankets over themselves against the cold night airs and woke in the morning stiff and cramped and unwilling to release those cramped muscles without a good deal of complaining. Someone would go off and find some food, fresh fruit, figs, dates, some fresh baked bread and goat's milk and bring it back for all to share before they went down into the city again where, as the Gospel writers rightly state, the people flocked to listen to Him in the temple.

At this point in history, 2000 or so years after the event, that seems a perfectly logical statement. Behind it lies a whole host of contradictions and strange happenings.

The Temple was there for preachers and teachers. There was a nice clear space where he had thrown out the moneychangers and sellers of sacrificial animals, they had shifted themselves elsewhere and carried on their trade – if there is money to be made, people will make it, no matter what - and this rough looking, long haired, bearded person now sat in the space on a stone ledge and talked to the crowds who came to hear him. He talked of simple things, as he had done on his journeying round the Sea of Galilee and across Judaea for these were still simple people and needed simple preaching to reach into their hearts. At the back of the crowd would stand the richly dressed lawyers, scribes and Pharisees, listening, absorbing, planning and scheming. They wanted him out. They wanted the temple back the way it was, with the pious coming and changing their money and dropping that money into boxes for them to collect later and pilgrims buying sacrificial animals and doing all the things they had been doing for many, many years without let or hindrance – until this man came along and stopped it all.

The pilgrims who should have been grateful to be there at all, who should have been in awe of the lawyers, scribes and Pharisees, who should have accepted their pronouncements as a total statement of the law, weren't doing anything they should. They were coming to the man called Jesus and listening to his words instead. And because His words made more sense, they took no notice of the others hanging around, went to no other rabbis for preaching.

The one thing he did not do at this time was attempt any clairvoyance. There were enough problems going on without him suddenly giving messages to people, so that was kept out of the equation. No, healing and preaching was all he and the disciples did but it was enough to keep the crowds coming back and coming back and coming back until we thought there would be no end to the people who came to listen.

They were there for the Passover, the great Jewish festival which has to be conducted with strict regard to the laws of Moses. And that feast time drew ever closer.

And the part of the story approaches that has had more misinterpretation than any other part of the whole of his life. Never has a man been more maligned than Judas Iscariot. His name has gone down in history as a traitor, a turncoat, a betrayer of friends.

I have said that Judas and Jesus walked nights together, talking, for Judas had been chosen to ensure that the prophesy was fulfilled. Night after night they talked, for Judas did not want to do this. He had great love for Jesus, a tremendous love, for he had given Judas a meaning to his life that he had been lacking. He was not an outstanding healer, he did not preach well but he did his share. He helped with keeping control of the money, he paid for food, he organised the supplies and the lodgings when he could. And he agreed, reluctantly to be the one who would betray Jesus, as no one else could be trusted to do the job. Any of the others would have said no and that would have been the end of the Plan.

No one noticed when he slipped quietly away to talk to the priests and temple police.

I wonder how Jesus did not throw the plan out himself. He only had to whisper to Simon Peter that Judas had taken money from the Chief Priests to turn him in – he had to do that, to make the event believable to the authorities - and the story would have had a vastly different ending to the one we all know, have believed in and have had at the centre of Christianity for these thousands of years. And who would have blamed him for putting a stop to it? Would we, any of us, willingly have gone ahead with our chosen destiny if we could have found a way to avoid it, found a way to walk another path for a time and gone home by a different route?

But in the face of coming death there is quiet acceptance of the fate that is to be. You see it in cancer victims, in those with serious heart conditions or leukaemia or any of the other terrible terminal illnesses you suffer on the earth plane. There comes a time when the patient stops fighting and sits back, saying 'what will be, will be, so let it happen.' This is Jesus at this time, weary of the travelling, the preaching, the constant pressures of finding new stories and new depths of courage to keep him going. It is a time when he said, 'let's get this done and done with, shall we?' in his heart and we knew it, we who walked with him. Even taking that into account, there was a very hard road still to walk and we would not have blamed him for turning His face away from Jerusalem, from Judas and all that waited for him and gone back to Nazareth.

Yes, I have said it before and doubtless will say it again before this chronicle of the extraordinary life is done.

And such is the intensity with which I am expressing these thoughts that, for the first time since we began the book, my channel has tears in her eyes. My emotions are coming out in her, for she has no reason to cry right now. She has music in her ears and nothing but my thoughts in her mind, so it is my thoughts, my emotions, which are causing the tears. I am not apologising for them, for this was by far the worst moment we had faced in the time we had spent on the earth plane. His feelings reached us and we in turn reacted to them, wanting to move in even closer than we were and comfort him. Judas returned and took his place among the disciples again, sitting at his feet, bringing him food and water, serving him as he had always done, without so much as a flicker of emotion showing of what he had done. But we know, from the guardian angel whose task it was to walk with Judas, that he too was hurting badly at that time, for only when the deed was done, the course of action sparked and set in motion and nothing, but nothing, could stop it. So Judas sat and cried inside, silently, desperately, wanting to turn back the clock. But a deed once done remains done. A word once spoken remains spoken, no matter how you might rationalise it, apologise and agonise over it. It is done. With Judas he knew it was done and he knew he was powerless to stop what would happen, he had to go through with it to the bitter end. And it would be bitter, the gall ate at his very heart even as he sat there and listened and spoke not a word. When he felt the loving eyes on him, it burned even more than the gall of his own actions. Why him? Why did he have to be the chosen one to ensure it went through? But he was and he did it and we knew it. We knew too that his name would be a disgrace for hundreds of years, until now, for this dear channel accepted Judas and wrote his story for him. He knew what was ahead, he knew the disgrace would affect him forever and yet he went through with it, for love of Jesus. No man had a greater love for him, we do believe.

From the hill outside Jerusalem, Jesus sent his disciples into the city to arrange the Passover meal. They were baffled, they had no home, they had no family to call on; where would they arrange such a thing?

His orders were very precise, we knew they had been worked out in advance for we had overheard and seen the arrangements being made but they didn't. It seemed like magic to them.

He told them to go the city and there meet a man carrying a jar of water. He said they were to follow the man into his house and say to the householder: 'he says, where is the room in which he can eat the Passover with his friends?'

Looking at each other with total bemusement, several disciples got up and walked off toward the city, wondering if he had finally gone over the edge, for surely such a thing would not and could not happen. But as they set foot in the city, so the man walked by carrying the jar of water. Even more baffled, they followed the man and entered a house they had never seen before and where they saw a man they had never met before and passed on the message.

In fact, the householder was someone who had been healed by Jesus earlier and had said, in his gratitude,

"Lord, if you have nowhere to celebrate the Passover, please feel free to use my home." And so the arrangements were made there and then, including the way the disciples would find the house, for directions alone would not have led them to this house, which was tucked away in a back street, where it was quiet.

The room was big enough, with sufficient chairs, so they set to and got the place ready for the Passover feast. Then Jesus came with the rest of the disciples and walked in as if he owned the place, taking his seat at the head of the table as if he had always been there. His quiet calm seemed to reach out to them all. Everything said this was not a normal Passover, something and everything had changed. The atmosphere was not exactly tense, not even really strained but there was an air about everyone, almost of expectancy, as if a great happening was about to take place. A solemn happening.

What they did not expect was the ritual with which he opened the meal, handing round the cup of wine and bidding them all drink of it 'as if in remembrance of me', breaking the bread apart and handing it to them, a piece at a time, 'as my body will be broken, so take this and eat it as if in remembrance of me.' They took what he gave them, solemnly, fearfully, reverently, wondering what other strangeness this Passover would hold.

They did not expect the next bombshell, though. Jesus suddenly put his hand on the table and said: 'my betrayer is here. His hand is on this table with mine.' There was silence, that kind of awkward silence that happens when someone commits an act that is irrevocably and implacably against all the known rules of good manners and social graces. Betrayer? What did he mean? Dare they ask? They didn't. To cover the embarrassment of the moment, they began another of their stupid arguments about who would be of a higher rank than the others. He called them to order and began to talk to them about the strength they would need and the trials they would face. Simon Peter, big as ever, leapt up and threw out his arms. "I will go with you to prison and death!" he announced.

Jesus took his arm and gently tugged him back down onto his seat. "Don't be so bold, Peter," he said softly, with the first hint of tears in his eyes. "Before the cock crows, I tell you that you will have denied me three times."

Simon set about denying it, bold and brash as always, but he hadn't reckoned on his clairvoyance that night. He hadn't noticed either that Jesus had nodded to Judas, a nod that said: 'I know, go about your business' and Judas slid quietly from the room without the others realising he had gone. We knew he had to, as Jesus did, as he did, for the Plan to be fulfilled.

Does that make Jesus sound like a pawn in a very big game played by Spirit? In some ways he was, for the Plan, the great scheme which was to bring a new religion to the whole world, was centred around him, without him it would not and could not happen. He knew it, too, which is why, despite all his feelings, he walked into that accursed city at that time, knowing the scribes and Pharisees were scheming to do away with him as soon as possible, for all they had built in the way of status and respectability was being chiselled away, story by story, parable by parable. The fact the moneychangers had not been allowed back into that section said a lot, too. They looked - and felt - foolish. They needed a grandstand finale to restore their position in society.

Let us not forget the role of the Romans at this time. This was not only a Jewish problem, but a Roman one, too. They did not want insurrection and upheaval, they did not want some wandering preacher defeating the best brains with deft answers to legal questions. It made them look silly. Suppression was everything and here was someone doing the exact opposite, rousing the people, getting them to think for themselves.

That in itself was enough to condemn anyone to death - in their eyes.

We divert. Yet again!

We left the disciples at the table with Jesus, wondering what the comment was all about, wondering what this business of betrayal really meant and this exhortation for strength and courage. No one dared ask, the whole meal had been so very different, with the strange ritual, the almost ominous words he had uttered and slowly, so very slowly, they began to piece together all the lectures and talks, all the 'I am going to Jerusalem to die' pieces began to slot together to form a picture they did not want to view. For how could they go on without him to lead them, leaderless they would surely falter and fall by the wayside! All that work, all that healing, all that preaching and walking and sleeping rough and living from hand to mouth and the raising of the dead and the driving out of the devils, all to go to waste? Panic is infectious, he knew it and so he held them with gentle talk, quietened their minds, gave them strength to face the days ahead.

Then they left the house, with thanks to the householder who knew nothing of the dramas which had gone on upstairs, and made their way back to the Mount of Olives where, at last, he gave way to His inner feelings.

Have you never questioned who the angel was who appeared from heaven to give him strength when he prayed those terrible heart-wrenching words: "Father, if it be thy will, take this cup from me. Yet not my will but thine be done." It was the first time anyone had acknowledged that I had been there. I watched over him as his sweat fell like blood to the ground and my tears mingled with his, for his devastating overwhelming fear had finally won out. All that strength, all that bravado, fails in the dark hours when the true future looks you in the face and you cannot bear to look upon it for it is more horrific than you ever imagined. So, while most of the disciples slept, worn out with their arguments, their own panicky thoughts and fears and only one remaining awake to hear the words and see me standing over him, giving him all the strength I could garner for him at that time, I poured out all that I could into his body and mind.

It must have worked for Jesus roused himself and went to wake the disciples, saying the time was short.

Indeed, even as he spoke, the crowd came to the hill and Judas was among them. It was then, for the very first time, the disciples realised that Judas had been missing from their group during the evening and night. Judas went to kiss Jesus but he stopped him. You do not betray someone with a kiss, but the sign had been given. Simon Peter swung at someone and cut off an ear but Jesus reached out and healed it immediately, saying: "let them have their way." He knew there was no point in arguing with any of them. They had their job to do and their job was his final walk to destiny.

They took him away. 'Arrested' is the word used in the New Testament, but it was no arrest for there was no formal warrant, just a bunch of soldiers determined to do their duty by the Temple in the hope of reward. A whole bunch of them for one man who walked the highways and byways with no weapons of any kind, no possessions and no home to return to. All those soldiers for one person. But he was not flattered, just afraid, humanly desperately afraid. Not that you would have known it from his face, the strength I poured into him helped Him keep his features perfectly calm, to encourage those around him.

The disciples followed down the hill, afraid, nervous, panicky. As Jesus was questioned by the Chief Priest, as the fists flew and the insults and questions were fired at him, Simon Peter was accosted by a maid in the courtyard who said "You were with Jesus the Galilean, were you not?" and in that moment, human instinct took over and Simon said "I don't know what you're talking about," and a small part of him shrank inside at the obvious lie. He got up and moved away, but someone else said the same thing and again he denied it. Then a third person approached him and again he denied it, at the very moment the cock began to crow for dawn.

In that moment Jesus' prediction flooded over him and he knew he had failed the first test. Tears streaming down his face, he stumbled outside and sat down, weeping.

Oh Simon Peter, how you have redeemed yourself since that time! A martyr's death, a glorious ministry, a whole church built around you and your famous keys! You had and have nothing to reproach yourself with, it was a human reaction and at that time you were all human, every single disciple, prey to human emotions and instincts and self-preservation is a powerful instinct. When you know someone you have worked with and walked with is being harangued before a court of lawyers and scribes, do you not lie to preserve yourself? Yes. It is natural, human and no more than anyone would have expected of you.

How do I know this, when I was in the court, watching him being punched, kicked, spat upon and insulted? The angel who walked with Simon Peter, who grieved with him outside the city wall, who gave him the strength to carry on, told me, for it was confirmation of his prediction and I liked to know that he had been right, not that I doubted! It is just proof; you know about that, you seek it all the time.

It is the same way I know what happened to Judas, his angel came to tell me when it was all over, how he had gone back to the priests and thrown the silver coins at them in his rage and disgust, partly at them, partly at himself. The words are wrong in the New Testament.

He actually said: “I have done a terrible thing and brought an end to a life that was innocent.”

And they said, as they would: “It’s out of our hands, you started something that cannot be stopped!” and they grinned their evil grins at him. If Satan was at work at all, it was with those men who sought an end to the Man of Galilee.

Such was his emotion at that time that he ran outside and, some time later, hanged himself from the nearest tree. But that is for Judas’ own book, not for this story,

But back to the so-called ‘court’.

They surrounded Him. They punched him in the kidneys, the back, the stomach. He staggered but never fell and never once did his face betray his feelings for them. He took every question and turned it so that it was they who said it, not he. They could not trick him into convicting himself. More fool them for thinking he would, after all their clever tricks had gone so drastically wrong in the years he had preached and healed around the area. They should have known better, but these were powerful men who felt threatened and would stoop to any depth to rid themselves of a troublemaker. They had no way of seeing the future, of knowing what result their actions would have on the world!

The tragedy moves on, irrevocably. There was an avalanche of emotion and dread inevitability about the whole thing which was very hard to bear, even for an angel. From the Jewish court to the Governor’s court and still he would not convict himself out of his own mouth.

Yes, he stood there proud and tall before Pilate, an unshaven, long haired man dressed in a simple robe, with dusty feet and calloused hands, roughened skin and an air of regality about him which did not go down well with those who watched. They wanted him to be humble, to beg for his life, to plead guilty and ask for clemency but he refused to do these things. He would not lower himself to do it.

Pilate could find no fault with him.

The crowd had been stirred up, money changing hands here and there, mob rule incited. It is easy to incite a mob; they follow a few leaders. There were many in the crowd who had heard Jesus and stood back, wanting nothing to do with the mock trial they knew was going on in the rooms above them. There were others, in the city for the festival, who knew nothing of what had gone on but were pleased to take a few coins and start shouting the name of someone they did not even know. Easy money: why turn it down?

Even as Pilate stood looking at the man before him, wondering how to get round the problem of dismissing an innocent man who had clearly got on the wrong side of the Jewish High Priest – which in turn boded ill for his relationship with the oppressed people if he did not go along with it – he heard the chant outside for Bar-Abbas.

He went to the balcony and looked down at the mob, holding up a hand for silence. When he got it, he asked: "who do you want released – Jesus of Galilee or Bar-Abbas?"

"Bar-Abbas!" came the shout. Such was the volume it did not appear that any in the crowd did not call out, but believe me, many did not. But, with so many who were shouting, it was not politic to go shouting for Jesus for fear of drawing the wrath of the mob on their head. We understood, we were there, we picked up their fear and sympathised.

And, we have to say, had it gone the other way, had the crowd for Jesus been more vocal, where then would the great Plan have been?

Pilate should have been a Solomon, he found the perfect way out. He called for a bowl of water, washed his hands in view of the entire crowd, called out "My hands are clean of this man's blood." And a great roar went up because then they knew they had won.

Ah, people of Jerusalem, may you forever be ashamed of your part in the great Plan, for you could have voiced a little opposition, shown a little sympathy, even perhaps not shouting quite so loud for the release of a rabble rousing murderer! Even at this distance of time and happenings, my heart can be turned over at the thought of the raw emotion spilling out that awful terrible day.

I saw his eyes for a single moment flicker with intense pain at the betrayal of so many after all he had done. But he knew, He understood the mob law, you go with the crowd or you die yourself. But it didn't make it any easier.

Sycophantic scribes clustered around Pilate. "You did the right thing, sir, this man is a troublemaker; he has roused the people to a fever pitch. He threw the money changers out of the temple; he has caused much dissent among the people."

Pilate was not to be calmed in this way. He knew, only too well, that he had committed a terrible crime and snapped at them. "Keep your nonsense for your own people. You know as well as I do that an innocent man just walked out of here to his death. Don't talk to me of rousing people to fever pitch. The man was calmness itself. I heard that he healed the sick and raised the dead. How much harm can there be in a man like that?" and he shut himself away for the remainder of the day, seeing no one and speaking to no one.

Pilate, you did but play your part in the great Plan. Yes, you could have gone against the mob, but it would have got you nowhere, for they were determined on doing away with him no matter what you did.

I hurried after Jesus. He was being hustled down to the dungeons where they stripped his robe from him, tied His wrists to a post and flogged him.

Not a sound did he make. Not once did he let them know the agony they put him through as they whipped him until the blood ran. His face was a mask of agony but no plea for mercy, for clemency, passed his lips. He let them have their fun. They dressed him in purple – not scarlet as was mentioned in Luke's Gospel, purple was the Roman colour at the time, rich, royal, they draped a cloak around him and someone bright spark went and plaited a crown of thorns which they forced onto his head, mocking the 'King of the Jews' indictment made against him. They mocked his miracles and his healing, telling him to escape from them if he could.

He could have. We could at any moment have stopped the heart of every person there and taken him straight to Heaven, back where he belonged. It would have taken just one word and we would have done it. Instead he looked at us with his sad smile and never said a word. Without permission we could not interfere.

So he stood there, back bleeding, agony shrieking through every part of him, thorns digging into his head, blood trickling down his face, hearing their mocking and receiving their spittle as they tried to humiliate and break his spirit. It didn't work. He stood like a king before them and in the end they gave up trying. There was no fun in trying to break someone who clearly would not be broken, no matter what they did. And anyway, time was getting short, there was a crucifixion to arrange.

Several, actually.

Your image of Christ dragging his cross to Golgotha is slightly – not much, but slightly – out of line with the reality of that awful terrible time. The cross was in fact in two parts and they forced the upright onto him to carry. He would never have lifted it had the cross-piece been in place, believe me, it was tremendously heavy. The carpenter, he who had the nails, carried or rather dragged the cross piece. The thieves, caught in the act and sentenced at the same time, dragged their uprights, too. The slow solemn procession began the long walk, Romans in front, guards to either side – as if a man was going to make off into the crowd after being flogged by the soldiers and treated like that! It was all they could do to walk, let alone try to run! He was in front, then came the two thieves, then came the carpenters and minions who always seem to be there, don't they? And then came the scribes, Pharisees, lawyers, those who were gloating that he had at last been stopped. After this they could go back to their way of life.

Somewhere in the background, following but staying part of the crowd, were the disciples, those who hadn't fled into the open land around Jerusalem. Simon Peter was there, crying inside, hurting, tears of remorse and guilt that he had let his Lord down, James and John were there, supporting Mary who had come to the city when the news reached her. All her fears had at last happened, all the secret worries she had harboured for so many years, all out in the open now. Blinded by tears, she staggered through the crowd, with James and John saying "this is his mother, let her through!" and pushing until they gave way. The crowds lined the streets because it was a spectacle. It wasn't they who were about to die. It was not their lives about to end in ignominy and unbelievable suffering. After this they could go home and tell people what they had seen.

And what had they seen? An innocent man, face dripping in blood but somehow still proud in his bearing, dragging a huge upright from a cross along the road, with Roman soldiers marching in front and Temple officials following up behind, sniggering and smirking when they looked at one another. Not to mention carpenters with nails and minions with cross pieces, all adding to the pathetic procession of humanity walking to its death. No majestic ending, this, no dignity except in his bearing, no sorrow except in his friends and family, no tears except those shed by his mother at this time. The others were hurting too much to cry.

And we walked the street with him, watched as he stumbled, watched the man come out of the crowd, a man with true compassion in his heart, and take the wooden stake from his shoulders and lift it as if it were matchwood. "Come, my friend," he said. "I know not what you have done but no man should suffer as you have." And he walked with Jesus to the hill and not one Roman or Jew tried to stop him helping.

There were more soldiers waiting there, jeering and calling insults to the three who were to die. The crosspieces were laid down on the uprights and nailed into place. Then the condemned were stripped and laid down on the uprights and nailed into place.

It was as casual as if someone were building a chair or a table. Gather the feet and put them on the small step, nail through them. Ignore the shrieks and screams of agony. Grab a wrist and hold it flat and nail through the hands, one at a time. Large pegs of wood and sharp nails. Then a whole bunch of soldiers grabbed the upright, lifted it and dropped it without ceremony or consideration straight into the holes which had been dug specially. His cross first, with its legend about being the King of the Jews, a nasty sarcastic notice, nailed to the top. Then the thieves, one each side, cursing and calling down imprecations on the heads of those who hung them there.

Mary pushed her way to the bottom of the cross, looking up at her son, tears pouring from her eyes so I am sure she saw nothing of his agony at that time. For surely she was blinded by her own tears. The disciples were with her, closely guarding her from the crowd who called and jeered at her for being there, for being so close.

"This is my son!" she screamed at them and they fell silent for a moment, understanding a mother's grief at seeing a son hanging shamefully on a cross above the city.

Questions you have all asked over the years.

Did the soldiers gamble for his cloak? Yes they did.

Did he say 'Father, forgive them for they know not what they do?' Not quite. It was "Father, forgive them for what they do." A small change in translation, a small change of words, a whole different meaning.

Did the soldier offer him the sponge? Yes, he did. A small merciful act, in some ways, for it contained a herb which was calming.

Did he forgive the thief who talked to him? Sorry, that one was entirely invented by those who wished to believe a conversation took place between people who were on the edge of asphyxiation, suffering deep traumatic shock, the most excruciating agony imaginable from first the nails and second hanging by them, every moment the flesh tearing a little more, the ribs folding in on the lungs, the heart fighting to stay pumping for a bit longer. No, there was no conversation for none could be had. All three were shocked beyond sensibility and lost in a fog of pain and despair verging on the unconscious all the time. Some took a long while to die that way; it was a cruel and sadistic way of killing people. Some lasted as much as six hours.

Did someone pierce his side? Yes, they did, to hasten the process. There were more to be executed, you see, and they needed the spaces, believe it or not.

Did he die on the cross? That's one you have asked many times, you who want to disbelieve the whole thing. Yes, he did.

Did it last just three hours? No, more than that. He lost consciousness after three hours, when he shouted out, as if in his dying moments 'It is finished!' but he lapsed into unconsciousness then from which he never recovered.

Did the sky cloud over? No, it didn't. It remained bright and clear and beautiful, a day on which no one should have died.

Did the temple veil tear? Not on its own. Someone, who shall remain nameless, tore it from top to bottom in their total despair at what was happening, someone who actually had a conscience about what was happening out there on Golgotha.

Did we cry, us angels? Yes, we did. We stood around the base of that hated hallowed Cross and cried helplessly, like human beings. As his mother did and his disciples and indeed some who stood around who knew of him but didn't know him, they cried too.

We knew and they knew by the way the body slumped on the cross that it was all over.

Then came the problem – burial. It had all happened so fast no one had thought about where, how, who and so on.

As they stood there, sorrowing, crying, panicking, a man pushed his way through the crowd and stopped in front of Mary.

"My dear lady." He took her hands and for a moment we all saw a brief flash of that smile, the one which had encouraged Jesus and others through the years. "I knew your son and I wish to offer you my burial tomb for him." Joseph of Arimathea, your name will go on forever throughout history for your loving gesture.

The soldiers lifted the cross down and prised the nails out of his hands and feet. Joseph wrapped the body in fresh linen and the disciples helped carry him to the tomb which was not that far away. It was cut into the rocks, with a large stone to roll across the entrance.

Here Mary said her goodbyes to her son, Simon Peter, James John and all the others who had gathered also said their farewells and rolled the stone into place, hurrying away to their shelter for the night for the

Sabbath was about to start and devout Jews were about to begin their devotions.

Life After Death

For you, the story ends here for three days.

For us it was a busy time.

His spirit had left him and was resting in the Summerlands, being healed from the wounds inflicted by the nails. Here he greeted those who had passed before him, He was reunited with John known as the Baptist, He recharged himself for there was still much work to be done.

While that was going on, we got the stone rolled away and the body moved.

Shock - horror! I can almost feel the reader reeling back at that statement, but I can assure you all it is perfectly true. We, Raphael and I, rolled back the stone and removed the body.

In Matthew's Gospel it says that there were guards at the tomb for fear of the disciples doing what we were about to do. Well, if there were, we didn't see them and they certainly didn't see us. My belief? Guards were posted but they went home, for who wants to sit outside a tomb?

Now you want to know what we did with the body. That, dear reader, is our secret and one that must remain a secret for all time, for you would all go digging for it if we said where we laid the bones.

Now you want to know why we did it.

Now we come to the real reason why he came in the first place and why he died as he did.

You all have eternal life. You all live on beyond the earthly body going to its rest in a grave. We can say that, we have said it for thousands of years, but – people had reached the point when they had to have it proved to them. Proof, something you all demand. He would be coming back to visit his disciples and others, to prove eternal life, but we needed to ensure that the proof was a thousand per cent believed. Are you with me so far? I hinted about this to my channel when we began the book and said I would explain in greater detail when we got there. Well, we are here and I am trying to explain.

Without a body they had to believe in eternal life, didn't they? So when he visited them in his spirit personality they could see him and accept him as risen from the dead. He had, in every sense, risen from the dead but we took the body to ensure that the belief was one thousand per cent believed.

Does this make sense to you?

It makes perfect sense to us, even after two thousand years.

He took the three days to rest, to recover, to draw on that inner strength that had sustained him throughout his earthly life. He walked and talked with those in the spirit realms and took in their wisdom and understanding to bring back with him, for he had to come back and complete his task. He got no further than the spirit hospital and rest place during that time.

So it got to be Sunday and the women came with their spices and their tears to attend to the beloved body. But it was gone; all they saw was me, sitting on the ledge, patiently awaiting their arrival.

"He's not here," I told them, as if they couldn't see that for themselves. Bit of a silly statement but at a time of grief and confusion, sometimes people need to be told the obvious. "He has gone on before you; he will see you all in Galilee."

That was the message he asked me to give for him. It baffled them for a while and I sat placidly waiting while they worked out a few things. First, there was no body. Second, they were speaking to an angel that they could clearly see. Third, that he had left a message for him, which surely meant that he was still alive.

The women left in a great hurry, rushing to tell the men what they had found. Within a very few minutes the disciples were there, rushing in to see for themselves that the body had gone and I still sitting patiently waiting. Oddly, they did not see me, perhaps not being as aware as the women. They left to go home, believing at last everything Jesus had told them about rising from the dead and living on. Only Mary remained, she who had loved him beyond all reason. And it was to her that he appeared briefly, telling her not to weep but warning her not to touch him. If she had, she would have known he was spirit and that would have confounded the whole illusion we were working so hard to preserve. But she was content to have seen him, it filled her heart with great joy and she went to tell the others what had happened.

Of course they didn't truly believe it. After all, the physical presence had gone; the driving force which had kept them all going had gone. For some, it had all ended with the misery of the cross, for others the faint hope that it was true lingered, for they knew of the empty tomb. Just as we planned it would … and they continued to gather together, for comfort, for easement of their sorrow and grief at being alone, without their leader.

It was on one such evening that he materialised in front of them. Appeared, it says in the Gospel, materialised is the right word for that is what happened. He was not there and then he was there, in the middle of the group, giving them his blessing, showing them his hands and, as they asked, his pierced side. Only Thomas was not there and he refused to believe until he saw it for himself.

One week later, he appeared again to the disciples, materialising strongly enough that Thomas could indeed put his finger into the holes made by the nails.

He visited his disciples many times during the days that followed, not always materialising but using only voice communication. He used this time to instruct them on how to go on, filling them with the Spirit fire that would take them out into the world to spread the gospel, the good news, that life is eternal and death had been conquered once and for all. The first circles then were set in place, for when they gathered together, so they created enough power that he could come and speak to them and be with them for a short while. Can you imagine the power that was going on then? These strong mediums, for everyone who sat was a medium in his own right and a healer, too, gathering in one place with the sole intent of bringing Jesus to them for further instruction! It was wonderful, I can tell you. The light that went up from those circles lit up the Realms and we were drawn to it, as he was. Magically, the light never went out after the circle dissolved for the night, but carried on as they went out to do his work.

It is a mystery to me even now that the Gospel according to John says that he only showed himself to his disciples three times. I can count more times than that, without including the voice communication ones. Did John not wish to admit that Jesus came to them in circle? Was he afraid of what others might say if they knew they communicated regularly? Did this first set of Spiritualists, even at that point, worry about what the public thought? Certainly the recorded times were spectacular ones, for the third time which is actually written down was when Jesus walked the beach and waited for Simon Peter and the others to come back from fishing, without fish that night, until he instructed them to drop their nets on the other side and they came up full.

That was the classic time when he, in his great unconditional love, gave Simon Peter the chance to redeem his thrice denial by asking him three times if he loved Jesus. Then they shared a breakfast which was more love than material food, a love that would sustain them through their terrible days ahead, for he knew, more than they did, that they too would be martyred for the sake of their faith. Then he left them to continue their fishing, their hearts full of happiness and joy.

He left them for he had another job to do – walking with the men on the road to Emmaus, teaching them the prophecies from Moses to date, showing how Jesus of Nazareth, he whom they mourned, had fulfilled the prophecies and had to die to go into glory. It was a wonderful sight, seeing their faces when the veil was lifted as they sat down to a meal and realised who their companion was. Even as he faded from their sight they were on their feet and rushing back to spread the good news of eternal life and his resurrection from the dead.

To confound everyone, he appeared there with them, showing them his body, his hands and his feet, even eating a piece of fish to prove his reality. The fact it was transposed into spiritual matter before he ate it is neither here nor there; they didn't see it, we did. It did much to settle their minds that this was not a ghost but a living person, which is what we had been aiming for all along.

Then he faded from their presence, returning to the Summerlands for another rest period before coming back yet again – but that goes into the next section.

Spreading the Word

For a while the disciples, those who were coming together to form the Brotherhood, were leaderless and directionless until the time the tongues of fire came. They did not know what was to come, only that he had promised them something which would help them carry on. The baptism of the Holy Spirit. They were told not to leave Jerusalem, which in itself was a hard thing to do, for they all had an abhorrence for the terrible place which had cost their friend his life. But his instructions were clear and they were used to obeying him in all things, so they waited.

The Twelve were one short, Judas having taken a short cut to the Summerlands and they felt they needed to replace him, to keep the Twelve intact. They nominated Matthias, a quiet spoken unassuming man with a devout and unshakeable faith to take his place. We approved; we let them go right ahead and make the nomination, knowing it was right.

And so there were Twelve to lead the Brotherhood into the new age of Gospel preaching and teaching across the land. But first, they needed the baptism of the Holy Spirit.

It happened suddenly, on the day now known as Pentecost, when a great crowd was gathered in one place. The power of so many strong-minded people together brought Spirit in with a rush as if it were a great wind. There was heat, as if flames sat on each one, but the heat came from each one individually, the power they were sending up. They were so filled with Spirit that they found themselves speaking in tongues and suddenly a crowd developed outside, for they could hear this and knew that inside were only simple Galileans. And those Galileans were speaking in their language. It was like a miracle, a gift from Heaven. Today you would know it as trance; these simple Galileans were speaking in tongues because they had been taken over at that time, at that moment, by their spirit guides and helpers. For those outside and indeed those within, none of this was known and the whole thing was a miracle to them. Apart from those who thought the disciples had been drinking.

The one thing that is absolutely right in the Acts of the Apostles is the fact that this happened at 9 in the morning, not in the evening when people would or could have been at the wine all day. Unlike you in this modern day who save circle sitting until the evening (because you have to, we understand that) they were sitting early because they were waiting for the sign from Spirit that the time had come to go out into the world. So Peter was able to make a statement refuting this drinking nonsense and give them a lecture on Jesus of Nazareth which shocked some, stunned others and left even more in total disbelief. And the call went out to repent.

This is something not known in the Spiritualist movement, the actual act of repentance. As we wrote that, my channel remembered from her dim past two occasions when she went to confession in the movement known as the Church of England. But the act of confession did not change her the way being in this movement has changed her, for now, each circle she sits, each service she attends she is drip-fed philosophy on changing your thinking, on living in harmony with others, both animal and human, of respecting all and most of all making allowances for others. Working with Spirit has changed her without the need for an act of repentance. But at that time, back then, this was a symbolic act, the giving up of the old thinking and taking on the new. It did not last; no one's thinking changes that completely but the seeds were sown, much as Spiritualists sow the seeds now.

The Acts of the Apostles give many examples of 'miracle' healing, spiritual healing, which stunned the people and confounded the elders. Arrested, thrown into prison overnight, dragged before a court of the Jewish rulers, so the martyrdom of the apostles began. But it did not stop the word spreading or people believing in the risen Christ, as it was planned to be.

The new church was beginning to grow. Each person who joined sold their property and made it a joint possession, becoming part of the whole. But not only physically – emotionally and mentally they became one and the great power of the Spirit was with them, filling them, guiding them. Peter and the other disciples were true mediums by then, with the power to see through deception and greed, so when the man known as Ananias came with only part of his money to offer, the shock of knowing his double dealing had been seen so clearly caused his heart to stop. Simple as that. Shock can stop a heart beating, it did with him. As it did with his wife, too.

These were sad things but went to prove to those around that this church, this embryo movement started by the man we chose to serve was going in the right direction. It had power, it had authority and it had the backing of the common people. That in itself made it dangerous to those in authority, for once again their rule was being challenged, just when they thought they had done with the 'trouble maker'.

The part of the Temple known as Solomon's Cloister was their meeting place, these men of God. To them came the sick, the diseased, the possessed and all were cured.

Call in the angel cavalry. Arrested and shut up in prison yet again, (Acts of the Apostles 5, check it out!) I went and opened the door for them and said "get out there and start healing and teaching again! We have need of you!" and confounded them all by locking the door after them so the officials who went to the prison found the doors locked and the apostles gone. All right, locking the door was a bit of a mean trick, in a way, but it helped add to the mystery of these great men and at that time they were great men, taking on the mantle of the one who had taught them so well, without having his physical presence and his great power to help them, still they battled against all opposition. It also amused me and that is a consideration, of course...

My channel is aware that this part of the book is not moving as swiftly or as smoothly as the earlier part and she is wondering if it something in her mind or mine. It is neither; it is the simple fact that the first part of this story was much easier to write for I was intensely involved from the moment he decided to return to earth. Once he had returned to his home in the Summerlands, my visits were rather more intermittent, as with opening the door to the prison and locking it again to confound everyone and amuse me. Much of what we are writing now was observed from the Summerlands with only rare visits back to earth, for my work was basically done. But there is one great momentous occasion of which to write and we are getting there, slowly but surely.

I wanted to give some idea of the work of the Apostles at that time, how they were empowered by the Great White Spirit of Love to carry on the work of spreading the Gospel, how the healing continued, even as much as Peter's shadow falling on them healed people, so great was the power of these devoted and loving men. It took more devotion and love to carry on in the face of being flogged and sent out into the world again for their wounds were sore indeed but they bore them proudly and carried on the work he had started.

It also says much for his power when on the earth that his followers carried on in this way and were not scattered to the four corners of their country, to hide until the furore had died down.

You will recall, dear reader, that we mentioned death by stoning earlier in this book, when it gave him whom we love a chance to be as wise as Solomon. If you read the Acts of the Apostles as far as we have gone now you will find a true death by stoning, that of the saint you know as Stephen. I will reiterate here that it is a terrible death. Each stone hurts, breaks bones, breaks skin, you do not know how long you will take to die, how much pain you will endure before you finally give up the earthly body. It is a horrendous death. Fortunately we were on hand to take Stephen swiftly home and to give an object lesson to a young man you and we knew then as Saul. For he stood there and approved of the murder of a young vibrant man who was filled with the love of God.

Every movement suffers persecution, the Spiritualist one is no exception to this rule, even now people would close the meeting houses if they could; they make the sign of the evil eye and other such superstitious nonsense as they pass by. After the death of Stephen, Saul led the persecution against the new believers, dragging people from their homes, throwing them into prison. I know his guardian angel very well. We have worked together over many hundreds of years. He had a very bad time with Saul then, trying to guard his charge but trying also to show him the error of his ways without success, for Saul was blinded by his own righteous fervour and few can get through that. You know this from the religious men you come up against time and again in your lifetime and on your earth plane. Your history books are full of them. One such was Oliver Cromwell. A religious man who stamped your country with the dread curse of Puritanism. Others were the terrible witch finders, condemning innocent women for mediumistic abilities or simply because they didn't approve of them. More were to be found in the terrible Inquisition. Religious people always have the shock of their deaths when they come to the Summerlands and often need a considerable period of rehabilitation before they can come to terms with their new surroundings!

So Saul's guardian angel was trying to open Saul's eyes but he wasn't having any of it. His mind was closed, tunnel visioned you would call it and iron-clad in its resoluteness. The angel went back to Jesus and begged for help. This he told me later, after the 'miraculous' happening. Few people can hold out against angel urging, angel guidance, angel direction but Saul had managed it, for his will was powerful in the extreme, which is why we needed him.

Not so much 'call in the angel cavalry' this time as 'call in the Higher Powers'. It would take nothing short of a miracle to move Saul and a miracle we schemed to create. I didn't know then of the plea, just that I had been called. We held a swift convocation of angels which he attended and agreed that his movement was in serious danger of breaking down, that this Saul had to be stopped – in a positive and constructive way. Oh it would have been easy to arrange a death, to bring him swiftly to the Summerlands and say 'look at him in all his glory and now say sorry!' but that was not part of the Plan. The Plan was to spread his word, to keep his movement alive, to keep his memory before the people and to get them to repent and come back to the Lord God. Killing Saul would not do that.

Spirit moved fast. Saul was riding fast and hard, trying to get to Damascus when we, with the one we love in the centre of our group, appeared before him on the road. The light was dazzling, to the point when Saul could hardly see. Jesus held up his wounded hands for all to see and said, in his deep rich loving voice, "Saul, Saul, why do you persecute me?"

The Gospels say Saul responded by saying "Tell me, Lord, who you are." The one word he didn't use was Lord. He actually fell from his horse and shouted, "Who are you!" Not a question as much as a statement, for this was a proud Roman, not just a minion. He came from a high born aristocratic family and thought Rome was the world and he was heir to it. So the statement was: “Who are you!”

He replied, in the same deep rich loving voice that penetrates the hardest heart and the strongest tunnel visioned mind: “Jesus, whom you persecute when you persecute those who follow me.”

Saul was blinded by the light. Those around him, servants and followers, were crying out “Master, what’s happening? Why do you speak? What is wrong with you?” for Saul was staggering around, unable to see, he who had been thrusting and boastful and full of vengeance against all who followed Jesus the Nazarene. And he could not tell them what he had seen and heard, for they would have thought he had gone mad. Indeed he thought he had gone mad. All he said was “A vision, a blinding light, has taken my sight. Help me!” Visions were something they understood so they took his arms and led him into the city.

We made him wait three days. The one we love waited three days to show himself to his followers, so we made Saul wait three days.

A whisper in the ear of a disciple named Ananias (yes, another one, it was a common name at that time…) told him to go to the house of Judas and ask for the man from Tarsus who needed healing and that only he could give it. Although he wanted to rebel against the instruction – he knew of the man from Tarsus’ reputation – he went, as we all do when Spirit speaks. He went to the house, asked for Saul and said, “I have come to heal you” and laid his hands on him. Immediately Saul could see. It was as instant as that and it was, in his mind, a miracle.

From that moment on he was converted to the cause of the followers of the man of Nazareth.

The rest, as they say, is history. Saul became Paul, an inveterate writer of letters to young churches, a tireless worker for Spirit, a healer, a preacher and, for many, a thorn in the side of authorities. Many times his life was endangered; many times his disciples saved him. Many letters were written, only some have survived and those that have are not a true picture of the young churches of that time but clear enough to give you an idea of what it was like to be part of the new flourishing movement. I need not reiterate the stories, they are there for the reading in many different translations, from the King James version which my channel loves for its deep richness and almost melodic language, to the modern translations.

But we in the Realms do appreciate that the Letters have created their own problems over the years, injunctions which were right at that time are not right for your modern world, yet some cling to them. Remember always, which many of your scholars do not, that Paul was writing as a Roman first, as a Christian second, for we cannot escape our background, our upbringing, no matter how hard we try. He was writing of the laws at that time, as they referred to the embryo churches and their new growing foundations.

Let me make a bold stand, after all, it is MY book, and say in the Realms there are no distinctions between male and female who serve Spirit. It is not a matter that ever bothers us. Yet it has torn your churches apart. Women have as much a role to play in serving the congregations as the men. In the Spiritualist movement, where my channel has found her 'home', there are more women than men serving the people and that is an indication of the balance that should be there but isn't in the Orthodox churches.

I will further state here, which will upset some people, I am sure, that it is not necessary to wear special clothes if you become a Minister of any religion. Those in authority wear a uniform to distinguish them from the public, that is something I accept, but doctors do not wear a special collar or shirt, nor should a minister of any kind. For you both, in your own way, tend to the human body and mind. A doctor does as much good psychologically as he/she does physically with pills, potions and prescriptions, in simply setting a mind at rest or easing a troubled thought. But they do not wear a special type of outfit.

He whom I love and whom I worship and serve never wore a collar, or a uniform, throughout his ministry. All that I would say is; be discreet in what you wear, so that what you wear does not distract from the message you are directed to give.

And so the story is ended.

My mission with him was over although I continue to walk with him at all times throughout the Realms, when I am not called upon to walk with a channel who needs a guardian angel to lead her through the wilderness into which her thoughts often take her. Again, I see her smile; she knows full well I am always with her. She also knows, for I told her just a few days ago, that I have been her guardian angel throughout her many, many incarnations. This seems to have pleased her immensely and I find that flattering. Archangel I may be, but I still like to think I am wanted and appreciated by my channel. Call it vanity, if you like, I say it is the 'human' side of me that makes me approachable - for some appear to be afraid of Archangels, for reasons I do not fully comprehend. They do, however, speak to me and that is good. Michael has his share of devoted admirers, as does Raphael and Uriel, but the other Archangels are not as well-known and are not called upon as much as we are. It is time for a change...

It is also time for some angel philosophy. The sad situation – and it is incredibly sad – in Northern Ireland

and in the once Holy Land are not obviously resolvable. We have watched with growing consternation and a good deal of heartache as the religious divide in Northern Ireland has driven a mile wide rift between people who should be living together, who speak a common language and share a common background and an equal right to the land on which they live and work and hate and die. This was not what He intended. He never meant you to fight over His words in this way. He never meant for there to be divisions of any kind. Peter was the Rock on which the church was to be built but as always, greed for power, for money, for status and for position crept in, took over and before long the church was rich beyond imagination and corrupt beyond anything anyone visualised. The church was to be for all, not for the select ones who could afford to be there. He brought a simple message that was extremely hard to live by – 'Love the Lord your God with all your heart and with all your mind and with all your strength and love thy neighbour as thyself.'

Try living by that creed, people of the earth, and see how quickly the divisions and dissents would fall away! Stop your children throwing stones; stop your young people creating bombs to kill others – and themselves. People of the Holy Land, save your young ones from the terrible death of being blown apart! The sadness, the grief, the hatreds being created there will last a thousand years unless something is done, unless someone is strong enough to say Enough!

And you will ask, rightly, why the angels aren't ready to interfere in these disputes and put a stop to them.

Once my channel got involved in a discussion with someone who is verging on atheism, for he was demanding to know why a child had not been saved. She has been cut to the heart by people around her bewailing the loss of an eleven year old girl and saying 'makes you wonder if there is a God' and she asked the first person, if you wish God to intervene and save EVERY child, no matter where or who, at what age do you stop saving them? Do you want God to say, 'I will save every child up to the age of 5, or 8, or 11' and forget the ones who are lost at 12, 14 and so on? At what age do you stop? And what of older people? Do you say 'fine, now you are 25, you are on your own, God will no longer save you from tragedy?' We have to say, it matters not what age you are, who you are, where you are, we cannot interfere with your karma, your life plan. If we could, we would have stopped the many civil wars, the world wars, the terror that was Cambodia, the nightmare that was Vietnam, the disaster that was Bosnia – I need not go on, surely, for the world, your modern world, is tearing itself apart and you know it, every rocket that is fired, every shot, every mass grave, every funeral.

If we were to physically stop the nightmare that was Northern Ireland, then we would have to stop the nightmare that is the Holy Land. And once we had done that, we would have to intervene in Macedonia, Afghanistan, Tibet … then someone would say 'but what about the rain forests and the melting ice caps' and we would spend all our time rushing around saving your world.

My dear readers, it is for YOU to save the world. It is for YOU, with prayers of peace and reconciliation, to bring about the change of heart that has to come before the change of mind, before people can sit down together and discuss their problems sensibly, calmly and quietly, with love and compassion for one another. Then, and only then, can the problems of the world be resolved, one at a time. If sufficient people want something strongly enough, then it will be done. The power of the mind is under-estimated, even now. YOU can do it. YOU as a community, as a country, as a people, can get together, all of you with one mind, and bring about change. If we were to do it, you would never take that great step forward which is the first great step to making your world one of a spiritual dimension.

It will come. It will happen because the Great White Spirit wishes it to happen. But YOU must be instrumental in doing it for your very own progression and that of your country and your world. It means not sitting at home, watching nightmare images on your television screens and then going to bed in the cosiness of your house and the comforting shelter of your own walls without offering a prayer for those who live in tents, doorways and war torn countries. See the images, weep over the images and pray for peace. Pray for it with true intensity, with true desire for it to happen.

2000 years ago a man was hung on a cross, a symbol of iniquity, of shame, of execution, of suffering and cruelty. That symbol has become the rallying cry, the focus of adoration, the very rock and foundation of a faith that has changed the world. One man.

Imagine what several million of you could do!

The story is told. My part in it is over. My lecture is complete. I have nothing else to say to you at this time, it is for your hearts and minds now to think on these things and create a solution which you have brought about.

It remains only for me to offer my thanks to my beloved channel for her time, her energy and her devotion to sit there and type these words. She has been at times amused, horrified, tearful, even a little shocked but through it all she has sat, with tingling hands and great love in her heart, to translate the words I have given her.

She is a fine worker for Spirit, much cared for in the Realms. There is much more work for her to do: this is far from being the only book she will translate. Already books are done and more are to come: the spirit who wishes to tell his story is standing by even as I write these final words.

My love and my thanks, dear sister, for recreating Living In The Shadow Of The Cross. You understand so much more now, can see how the story fits better when it comes with Spirit inspired background, to show why and how and when and where the events took place.

And now it is time for me to retire into the background, to carry on guarding this one I work with, to ensure she continues her work for Spirit as best she can. And I will work to get these words before the public, for they must be read and they must be understood. My channel has her instructions, which we have said before: no interviews, no statements, nothing that can be pounced on and twisted and distorted out of context. The words must stand alone for themselves, for they are nothing but the pure truth and as such are put before you, dear reader, in that way. The Truth shall make you free.

I wish you freedom, peace, contentment and most of all, love. Without that there is nothing.

That is one thing the Roman letter writer got right!

Afterword

The Archangel Gabriel adds these thoughts

It has taken some years to bring this book before the people. During that time an attempt, a serious one, has been made to bring peace to the troubled land of Ireland. The will of the people finally overcame the opposition of the politicians and they sat down together to discuss their differences.

And a new conflict flared in Iraq and took over the world's attention. Now that claims lives while the agony of Israel/Palestine continues, with death and destruction spilling into Jordan as well. And the whole area explodes into violence, whilst parts of Africa tear themselves to pieces, too.

It is to be asked by those of us sorrowing at this time if man will ever live in peace and the answer, sadly, is that we doubt it. There will always be a reason to fight and a reason to commit others to fight and die.

From the beginning of Time men have fought and women have mourned. Nothing changes. My channel's companion has a saying 'it was ever thus' and it is true. I would wish we could close this book with Good News but the only good news I can offer is the love of him who walked this earth and who brought the knowledge of everlasting life to the people in a way no other man has ever done – or ever will. We are grateful to the many mediums who work in the light, who stand the insults, the pure venom poured upon them, the vitriolic hatred shown to them by so many who refuse to understand they do his and God's will at this time.

As we write these words, my channel is reading my words on the page before this – 'the truth shall make you free.' A few days ago she added that to the very end of the paper she uses for letter writing. It seemed a strange thing to do, she thought, even as she did it. Now she knows why. It is the truth which needs to be put out there to everyone, no matter who, so it stays on the paper for her business letters as well as personal ones. It goes out with her motto – Amor Vincit Omnia – Love Conquers All.

Eventually it will.

Hold on to that great truth, dear reader, and do not despair.

Eventually it will.

These are the words of Gabriel, Archangel and servant to Jesus of Nazareth and the great all-seeing, all-powerful God of All. Guardian and friend of my channel, to whom I give all thanks and love for the work of getting this book to the world. Dear one, know I am with you always. And thank you for commissioning the portrait. It is good that the world knows how handsome I am…!

www.ingramcontent.com/pod-product-compliance
Ingram Content Group UK Ltd.
Pitfield, Milton Keynes, MK11 3LW, UK
UKHW020224250726
13967UKWH00001B/168

9 781904 086659